Murder at Howard Johnson's

A Comedy in Two Acts

by Ron Clark and Sam Bobrick

A Samuel French Acting Edition

New York Hollywood London Toronto

SAMUELFRENCH.COM

ISBN 978-0-573-61202-2 Printed in U.S.A. #730

OPENING NIGHT MAY 17, 1979

JOHN GOLDEN THEATRE

A Shubert Organization Theatre

Gerald Schoenfeld, *Chairman* Bernard B. Jacobs, *President*

Lee Guber & Shelly Gross

present

Tony **Roberts** Bob **Dishy**

Joyce **Van Patten**

in

a new comedy by

Ron Clark and Sam Bobrick

Directed by

Marshall W. Mason

Scenery Designed by **Karl Eigsti**

Costumes Designed by **Sara Brook**

Lighting Designed by **Richard Nelson**

Associate Producers **David S. Newman and Fred Walker**

General Management **Theatre Now, Inc.**

CAST
(*in order of appearance*)

ARLENE MILLER . . . . *Joyce Van Patten*

MITCHELL LAVELL . . . . *Tony Roberts*

PAUL MILLER . . . . *Bob Dishy*

ACT ONE

Scene One: Room 514. A week before Christmas.
Scene Two: Room 907. The 4th of July.

ACT TWO

Room 1015. New Year's Eve.

MURDER AT THE HOWARD JOHNSON'S premiered at the Golden Theater in New York City, May 17, 1979, directed by Marshall W. Mason, and with Tony Roberts, Bob Dishy and Joyce Van Patten among its cast.

CAST

(*in order of appearance*)

ARLENE MILLER . . . . *Joyce Van Patten*

MITCHELL LOVELL . . . . *Tony Roberts*

PAUL MILLER . . . . *Bob Dishy*

The play takes place in a Howard Johnson's Hotel somewhere in America. The time is the present.

CHARACTERS

(*in order of appearance*)

ARLENE MILLER

MITCHELL LOVELL

PAUL MILLER

Murder at the Howard Johnson's

ACT ONE

Scene 1

PLACE: *Room 514. A Howard Johnson's hotel.*
TIME: *Mid December. Evening.*
AT RISE: *It is a typical blue and orange Howard Johnson hotel room, with the usual hotel furnishing. Upstage, there are three windows side by side. The middle window has a desk and chair in front of it. The Stage Left window has a dresser. All three windows pivot on their centers, in frames. The bed unit is at Stage Right and includes two small bed tables on each side. One table has a telephone. There are two doors, Stage Right. The furthest Downstage is the closet door, the other, the bathroom door. The front door to the room is Stage Left. Between the bed and the front door is a floor lamp and two armchairs. There is a Christmas wreath on the headboard. A shopping bag filled with Christmas presents is on top the dresser. A TV on a stand is Downstage Left. In the background, we hear Christmas music.*

ARLENE MILLER, *an attractive woman, is seated on the bed, almost madonna-like, obviously troubled. From the bathroom we hear the bathtub water running for a few beats and then being turned off. Another beat or two and then the bathroom door opens and* DOCTOR MITCHELL LOVELL *enters.* MITCHELL *is a dentist and a contemporary of* ARLENE'S. *He's wearing a rather loud plaid jacket.*

MITCHELL. Well, the bathtub is ready. (*He goes Downstage, and brushes his hair in front of an imaginary mirror.*) What's the matter, honey? You're not nervous, are you?

ARLENE. I was just thinking, Mitchell. This is going to be the first Christmas in thirteen years that Paul and I won't be spending together.

MITCHELL. You've got to stop thinking about it, sweetheart. You've got to keep your mind on what we're doing.

ARLENE. If only he didn't love me so much. It would be a lot easier if he didn't love me so much. But, oh, God, how he loves me.

MITCHELL. (*Sits down on the bed next to her.*) He doesn't love you any more than I do.

ARLENE. Of course he does. He loves me more than any woman deserves to be loved.

MITCHELL. Well, if he loves you so damn much, why don't you stay with him?

ARLENE. You're jealous.

MITCHELL. Of course I'm jealous. I never felt this way before. I can't stand the thought of anybody but me touching you. I'm a dentist, Arlene. You know I can have any woman I want. But all I want is you.

ARLENE. Oh, Mitchell.

MITCHELL. I never told you this before, but remember when I put in that bridge for him and he went home in terrific pain? I purposely did that to him. I put in the wrong sized bridge. I wanted to hurt him.

ARLENE. I love you, Mitchell. (*They embrace passionately.*)

MITCHELL. I've got to have you, Arlene.

ARLENE. No please, not now. (*Rises.*) I've got too much on my mind. I wouldn't be any good.

MITCHELL. You may be right. (*Rises.*) Okay, let's go over the plan once more. One, I open the door.

ARLENE. Two. I say, come in, Paul, and don't ask any questions.

MITCHELL. Three. I hit him over the head with a lamp.

ARLENE. Four. I give him a karate chop in the neck.

MITCHELL. Five. I hit him over the head with a chair.

ARLENE. Six. I shove a handkerchief in his mouth so he won't scream.

MITCHELL. Seven. I give him the injection and he sinks to his knees. (*They heighten the pace.*)

ARLENE. Eight. We drag him into the bathroom.

MITCHELL. And nine, we dump him into the bathtub face down and hold his head under water for as long as it takes.

ARLENE. (*Embracing* MITCHELL *excitedly.*) Kiss me! Kiss me! I've got to have you, Mitchell.

MITCHELL. Not now, Arlene. You wouldn't be any good, remember? (MITCHELL *goes into bathroom.*)

ARLENE. Poor Paul. He's going to hate this so much. But what about me? Am I not entitled to life? Don't I deserve to know tenderness, warmth and passion without having to get up in the middle of the night, get dressed and take a taxi home? (MITCHELL *comes out with a doctor's bag.*) Oh, Mitchell, I don't know if happiness will ever be in the cards for a woman like me.

MITCHELL. We've got to think positive, Arlene . . . Where the hell is he? He said he'd be here at six.

ARLENE. Not if he's in the middle of a deal. You know when you're selling used cars, you can spend a whole day promising a guy the moon.

MITCHELL. I know. I bought my mother's Oldsmobile from him. The day after the warranty expired the motor fell out.

ARLENE. Paul used to tell me after he had a few beers that when you buy a used car, you're buying somebody else's troubles.

MITCHELL. Well, I'm getting even this time. He thinks he's coming up here to make a deal on some stolen cars.

ARLENE. I used to love him. I think I used to love him more than he loved me. Then suddenly things started to reverse themselves. I found myself being loved more than I could love in return. Do you have any idea what it's like being loved more than you can possibly love in return?

MITCHELL. Of course I do.

ARLENE. It drives you crazy. So you force yourself to love that person more than you do and before you know it you hate him for putting you through all this. Do you know what I'm saying?

MITCHELL. Thoroughly. God, when you two first came into my office to have your teeth checked, I would have sworn you were the happiest couple on earth. (*Closes the drapes.*)

ARLENE. (*Primping in Downstage imaginary mirror.*) When I met Paul Miller, I was young, I was foolish, I was innocent . . . But then I started reading. At first newspapers. Then magazines . . . and suddenly, before I knew it, books. Little by little, I outgrew him. He went to the right, I went to the left. He went in. I went out. I went up. He went down. I went here, he went there . . .

MITCHELL. I couldn't live with a man like that.

ARLENE. Yet, he tried his best. He gave me everything. A house, furniture, clothing, silverware . . . I have five watches.

MITCHELL. No one needs five watches.

ARLENE. Of course not. Oh, sure, Paul and I were happy at first. I didn't know any better. My eyes were still closed. I hadn't awakened as a person yet. And then when I met you, the whole thing really crystalized. I wasn't the same girl that Paul had slept with thousands and thousands and thousands of times.

MITCHELL. Arlene, I don't want to hear numbers.

ARLENE. Mitchell, he still is my husband.

MITCHELL. Well, that's all going to change today.

ARLENE. Kiss me. Kiss me. (*They kiss passionately. There is a knock at the door.*) That's him.

MITCHELL. Bad timing.

PAUL. (*Offstage.*) Mr. Zapata!

MITCHELL. (*Fake voice.*) Uno momento! (ARLENE *looks at* MITCHELL *puzzled.*) I told him on the phone, I was Mexican.

ARLENE. You have a very good accent.

MITCHELL. Thank you.

ARLENE. (*Goes to him.*) Oh, Mitchell. I can't help but wonder. Do we really have the right to take another person's life?

MITCHELL. Of course not. That's why it's called murder. You want total happiness, don't you?

ARLENE. Yes, yes.

MITCHELL. Well, he's keeping you from total happiness.

ARLENE. I'm so confused.

MITCHELL. Look, would it make you feel any better if we tried talking to him first? Who knows, he might even agree to a divorce.

ARLENE. Never. The poor guy loves me too much.

MITCHELL. Let's try. If he says no and we have to kill him, at least we'll have a clear conscience. (*There is another knock at the door.*) Uno momento! (*To* ARLENE.) What do you say, Arlene?

ARLENE. Okay, we'll try it, but don't get your hopes up.

MITCHELL. I love you, Arlene.

ARLENE. I love you, Mitchell.

MITCHELL. Think positive.

(*He turns on more lights in the room, opens the door and stands behind it.* PAUL MILLER, *a man a year or two older than his wife, is standing there. He is wearing a grey overcoat, a grey suit, and a grey tie. When he sees* ARLENE *he is completely confused.*)

PAUL. Arlene!?!?

ARLENE. Come in, Paul, and don't ask questions.

PAUL. (*Entering.*) Arlene, what are you doing here? I was supposed to meet a Mr. Zapata.

MITCHELL. (*Closes door.*) Hi, Paul, how's business?

PAUL. Doctor Lovell! What's going on? Where's Zapata?

MITCHELL. I'm Zapata.

PAUL. You? You're our dentist. You don't make enough money overcharging us? You have to operate a stolen car ring, too?

ARLENE. Paul, give me your coat. Dr. Lovell has something to tell you. (*To* MITCHELL.) Go ahead, honey. (*She takes* PAUL'S *coat and hangs it up.*)

PAUL. Honey? Who calls a dentist honey?

MITCHELL. Paul, here's the story. I love your wife. Your wife loves me. We're all adults. These things happen. What more can I say?

PAUL. You mean there are no hot cars?

MITCHELL. (*To* ARLENE.) You talk to him.

ARLENE. Paul, I want a divorce.

PAUL. A divorce!

MITCHELL. What do you say, huh, Paul? A nice clean split. We let the lawyers handle everything, we stay friends, and from here on in, all your dental work is fifty percent off.

PAUL. A divorce? I don't understand, Arlene. I'm really thrown. Just the other night we had sex like it was gangbusters. (MITCHELL *gives* ARLENE *a look.*)

ARLENE. (*To* MITCHELL.) I thought it was going to be his last time. I tried to make it special.

PAUL. (*Sits on foot of bed.*) A divorce!

ARLENE. What about it, huh, Paul! Yes or no?

MITCHELL. Otherwise we have to get rough.

PAUL. (*Stunned, to* ARLENE.) You and Doctor Lovell are in love?

ARLENE. I'm afraid so.

PAUL. In love with a man who butchered my mouth. It still hurts from that lousy bridge he put in.

MITCHELL. So don't pay me.

PAUL. (*Rises.*) I didn't.

ARLENE. Fellas, please . . .

PAUL. I can't believe it, Arlene. After all we've meant to each other. (*To* MITCHELL.) I love that woman. I treat her like a goddess. Whatever she wants, I get for her. You know, I bought her . . .

PAUL and MITCHELL. Five watches.

PAUL. I'd buy her anything. You know that, Arlene. Name me one thing you want that you haven't got.

ARLENE. Happiness.

PAUL. Arlene, you're talking about a very small part of life. I've failed you, haven't I?

ARLENE. No, Paul, it's not that simple. It's just that . . . well, some people change.

PAUL. (*Proudly.*) I didn't.

MITCHELL. Well, some people change and some people don't.

ARLENE. What I'm trying to say, Paul, is simply that it's not there anymore. The magic, the violins, the sunsets . . . the rain on my face, the moonlight walks . . .

MITCHELL. (*Sighs.*) I love all that stuff.

PAUL. I'm stunned. I'm really stunned. Why, Arlene, why? What's the real reason? Where did I go wrong? Was I too strong? Too weak? Too lenient? Too strict?

ARLENE. It doesn't matter now. It's all yesterday's news.

PAUL. What do you mean yesterday's news? I just found out about it. I have to know. Is it because I have no sense of humor?

ARLENE. No, of course not. A wife doesn't have to laugh all the time.

MITCHELL. (*Interested.*) Then what is it, Arlene?

ARLENE. (*A little annoyed.*) I met you.

MITCHELL. Of course.

PAUL. (*Sits again.*) I'm stunned. I'm really stunned.

MITCHELL. Oh, come on. You mean you didn't suspect anything? Your wife goes to a dentist two or three times a week, sometimes even on Sundays, doesn't come home till midnight and you don't suspect anything?

PAUL. I trusted her.

ARLENE. He was good that way.

PAUL. (*Rises.*) Something is wrong here. You're keeping something from me. A woman doesn't walk out on the perfect husband without a reason.

ARLENE. There are a lot of reasons, Paul. You're shallow. You're dull. You're gloomy. You never smile . . .

PAUL. You have a good memory.

ARLENE. The other day I went into your closet. Did you know your entire wardrobe is grey? You go into Mitchel's closet, there's color, there's life. There's reds and greens and yellows . . .

MITCHELL. And plaids and checks and stripes . . .

ARLENE. There is adventure in Mitchell's closet, excitement, a lust for life.

MITCHELL. I've got wide lapels, narrow lapels, flared pants, pants with cuffs. You name it. I'm ready for all fads.

PAUL. Doctor Lovell, what the hell kind of a man goes around stealing wives?

MITCHELL. Put yourself in my place. You're a perfectly healthy, normal, good-looking, dentist. An attractive married woman walks in one day, sits on your chair, you start examining her. Before you know it you're having drinks together and the rest is history.

PAUL. (*To* MITCHELL.) My respect for you has hit a new low.

MITCHELL. So don't recommend me.

PAUL. I never do.

ARLENE. Paul, I'm only flesh and blood. You expected too much of me.

PAUL. I expected you to behave like a wife. Didn't I satisfy you sexually?

ARLENE. Sometimes you did and sometimes you didn't.

PAUL. And you don't call that a good batting average? Arlene, marriage is like baseball. Sometimes you pitch. Sometimes you catch. Sometimes you hit a home run.

Sometimes you strike out. Sometimes you go into extra innings. Sometimes it's called on account of rain. But the sport goes on year after year after year after year.

MITCHELL. (*Interested.*) And then what?

PAUL. And then it's football season . . .

ARLENE. Paul, I'm not happy with you.

PAUL. I'm going to pretend I didn't hear that.

ARLENE. Of course you didn't hear that. You don't listen. Mitchell listens. He's interested. He cares. He wants to know what makes me tick. There are lots of things bothering women like me these days. Things that seem unanswered in our lives.

PAUL. Like what? I'll answer it.

ARLENE. Like what makes us feel so restless? What makes us feel so incomplete? What makes us feel so lost?

PAUL. Who can answer all that?

ARLENE. At least with Mitchell at night when I talk, he doesn't fall asleep.

MITCHELL. How can you possibly fall asleep with this woman next to you?

PAUL. I'm tired. Marriage takes a lot out of a person.

MITCHELL. Take time to smell the roses, Paul?

PAUL. Shove the roses. (*To* ARLENE.) You don't think I was disappointed from time to time in our marriage?

ARLENE. Like when?

PAUL. There were times. Lots of times. Like reading in bed all night long with the lights on. That bothers me. You always leaving the table before I finish eating. That bothers me. Some of the phone calls you take in private. That bothers me. Your using all my wooden hangers . . . I could go on and on.

MITCHELL. I really think this is getting too personal.

PAUL. I know his kind, Arlene. He's going to break your heart. He meets too many women in his line of work.

MITCHELL. Oh, yeah? Well, in fifteen years of medical practice, I've only had three affairs with married patients.

PAUL. You hear that?

ARLENE. He's only human, Paul. I admire that in a man. You, you never even looked at another woman. That's not natural.

PAUL. Why should I look at other women? I hate women.

MITCHELL. Well, I love women, and I especially love Arlene.

ARLENE. Did I get lucky, Paul?

PAUL. Look, Lovell, I know what Arlene is to you. A quick jump in the sack. A wham bam, thank you ma'am. Love is a lot more than pretty words. You single guys make me sick. Love! What do you know about love? What have you bought her in the last month?

MITCHELL. What do I know about love? That's a laugh. Who's winding up with Arlene, you or me?

PAUL. That's not love. That's sex.

MITCHELL. Sex *is* love.

PAUL. Sex is sex. *Love* is love.

ARLENE. I think basically you're both saying the same thing.

PAUL. Arlene, you don't think I could have affairs? There are women coming to buy cars all the time. All I have to do is knock two hundred dollars off the sticker price and I'm in business. But I'm loyal. And as long as there's an ounce of breath left in this body, you're going to be loyal too. Get your coat! (*He gets his coat.*)

MITCHELL. Paul, for the last time, are you or are you not going to give Arlene a divorce?

PAUL. Never. Get your coat. (MITCHELL *and* ARLENE *look at one another.*)

MITCHELL. Well, we can't say we didn't try.

ARLENE. (*Goes to door, takes the "Do Not Disturb" sign and places it on the outside of the door. She then locks the door.*) Paul, what happens from here on in is your own doing.

PAUL. What are you talking about?

ARLENE. Do you want to tell him?

MITCHELL. No, you tell him.

ARLENE. Okay, Paul, as cruel as this may sound at first, and as cold blooded as it may appear and as callous as . . .

MITCHELL. (*Impatient.*) Tell him already!

ARLENE. (*Her arm around* PAUL.) We're going to kill you, Paul.

PAUL. Say that again.

MITCHELL. We're going to kill you, Paul. (*He pulls out a white dentist jacket from his bag and proceeds to put it on.*)

PAUL. (*A beat. Looks at them.*) Get your coat, Arlene.

ARLENE. We're serious, Paul. We're going to kill you.

PAUL. Don't make me laugh.

MITCHELL. She's not kidding, Paul. The party's over.

PAUL. (*Chuckling.*) Let me get this straight. You're going to kill me? You two amateurs are going to kill me?

MITCHELL. We're amateurs now, but when we leave here we'll be seasoned veterans.

PAUL. This, I gotta see.

ARLENE. You don't think we're going to do it, huh?

PAUL. I don't think you're going to do it. I don't think you can do it. You think it's easy to kill someone? To stop their hearts from beating? To take their life away? People like us don't go around killing people. We're much too middle class for that.

MITCHELL. Who the hell are you calling middle class? I'm a professional dentist with diplomas all over the wall.

PAUL. You want to kill me? Okay, go ahead and kill me. What do you want me to do, sit in a chair while you tie me up? (*Takes off his coat and hangs it up.*)

MITCHELL. Well, we really weren't going to do it that way, but it's not a bad idea.

ARLENE. No, not at all. Thank you, Paul. (*Pulls chair to Center of Stage.*) Listen, you sit right here. I'll be right back. You'll see how cleverly we planned this whole thing. I think you're going to get a kick out of this. (*To*

MITCHELL.) Don't kill him till I get back. (*She exits into the bathroom.*)

PAUL. (*Sits in chair.*) Come on. Tie me up. Let's kill me.

MITCHELL. All right. What's the catch?

PAUL. (*Rises.*) I don't think you can do it. I don't think you have the guts. If you can, go ahead. But if you can't, then Arlene walks out of here with me, and we get a new dentist.

MITCHELL. Leave it to a used car dealer to come up with a scheme like that.

PAUL. Have we got a deal?

MITCHELL. You're on. (*They shake hands.*) Have a seat. (PAUL *sits down again.* MITCHELL *takes his own tie and begins tying* PAUL's *hands behind his back and to the chair.*)

PAUL. You know what my wife's problem is? It's those damn women's magazines she reads. They're too honest. They confuse her. They make sex look like a fun thing.

MITCHELL. (*Finishes tying* PAUL's *hands.*) Is that too tight?

PAUL. No, it's fine.

MITCHELL. I'm going to have to borrow your tie.

PAUL. Take it. I've got a dozen more just like it. (MITCHELL *removes* PAUL's *tie and begins tying his feet to the chair.*) Maybe it's her age. You know how women are about losing their youth. It's tough on a woman when she hits thirty-eight.

MITCHELL. (*Stops and reacts.*) She's thirty-eight?

PAUL. Didn't she tell you?

MITCHELL. I didn't know she was thirty-eight. How do you like that. I'm two years younger than her.

PAUL. Does that mean it's all off?

MITCHELL. Of course not. But why would she lie to me?

PAUL. People lie. They lie to each other. Sometimes on the lot I even have to do it. Me, Honest Paul Miller! All life is a lie. When you're a kid they tell you there's a Santa

Claus, that there's a pot of gold at the end of the rainbow. They tell you if you work hard, you'll be a success, if you find the right woman, you'll be happy. I'm living proof that everything's a lie. Everybody shafts you. But unlike Arlene, I've learned to live with it.

MITCHELL. At times, Paul, you come off as a very bitter person.

PAUL. I'm not bitter. I'm just realistic. I know that . . . (*Winces in pain.*) Oooooow!

MITCHELL. What's wrong?

PAUL. It's that lousy bridge you put in.

MITCHELL. (*Goes to bag and gets some dental instruments.*) Here, let me have a look.

PAUL. No, no. It's all right.

MITCHELL. Open wide. (*Looks into* PAUL'S *mouth.*) Have you been using your water pik?

PAUL. Who's got time?

MITCHELL. You're lucky you're going to die, Paul. You need twelve hundred dollars worth of work there.

PAUL. I wouldn't go to you if you were the last dentist on earth.

MITCHELL. Paul, for you, I am the last dentist on earth. (*The bathroom door opens and* ARLENE *comes out wearing a floozie wig.*)

ARLENE. (*To* PAUL, *playing a sexy hooker.*) Hello, big boy. You want to have some fun?

PAUL. What the hell is this?

ARLENE. It's me, Paul, Arlene.

PAUL. (*Annoyed.*) I know it's you.

ARLENE. This is how I registered downstairs as Kitty Latour. So that when they find your dead body, they'll connect it to this girl. (*Points to herself.*)

MITCHELL. You really look sexy in that wig.

PAUL. I think she looks cheap. She looks like a hooker.

ARLENE. Of course. That's what I'm supposed to be.

PAUL. You would associate my death to a hooker?

MITCHELL. It's the perfect crime. You came here to meet this hooker, you had sex in the bathtub, you hit your head and you drowned.

PAUL. Sex in the bathtub? And how will you explain my being tied to a chair?

ARLENE. Grow up, Paul. There are people who have sex like that every day.

PAUL. (*Shocked.*) Every day? What a world!

MITCHELL. The bathtub's all filled with water and all we have to do is drag you in there and dump you in, face down. (*To* ARLENE.) Then you and I can go out and get something to eat.

PAUL. Why don't we order something up?

ARLENE. (*Goes to phone.*) Great idea. Ever since we thought of killing you at Howard Johnsons, I've had a taste for fried clams.

MITCHELL. Arlene, hang up.

ARLENE. You love ice cream. They have twenty-eight flavors.

MITCHELL. I had my desert. I had a Milky Way before I came up.

PAUL. A Milky Way. What a baby. (*Taunting.*) You're a baby. Little baby . . .

MITCHELL. Hang up, Arlene. We'll eat when we're finished. Maybe I'll even take you dancing.

ARLENE. (*Into phone.*) Never mind. We're going to go dancing. (*Hangs up.*)

MITCHELL. I love dancing, Paul. I just love it. (*Starts dancing.*) One two, One, two, three.

PAUL. Well, I hate it. I'm on my feet all day, all night . . . Why should I want to dance? I want to sit and relax.

ARLENE. Well, I didn't. That's what ruins marriages, Paul, more than anything else.

PAUL. What? Not dancing?

ARLENE. No, not doing things together!

PAUL. Okay, so we'll do things together.

ARLENE. It's too late. You are who you are and you've gone as far as you can go. The big difference between us, Paul, is that you're tied down and I'm free. I've found myself. You didn't even go out looking.

PAUL. Arlene, I work twelve hours a day, seven days a week. I don't have time to find myself. You think I'm doing it for me? I'm doing it so I can buy you things. I don't need anything. All I need are shoes so I can continue to work to buy you those things.

ARLENE. Paul, you'll never understand. The basic fact is that I've outgrown you. I've matured. I've blossomed.

MITCHELL. That reminds me, Arlene. He said you were thirty-eight.

ARLENE. Paul, you're a very petty person.

MITCHELL. Do you think I care about age? Nobody cares about age anymore.

ARLENE. You're as young as you feel. And I feel like a spring bride. I want to go. I want to do. I'm restless. I can't be contained. I want to write. I want to paint. I want to take ballet lessons. I want to go around the world.

PAUL. (*To* MITCHELL.) Doctor Lovell, do you have any idea what that's going to cost you?

ARLENE. I've spent too many years just sitting around waiting. Waiting for something to happen. Waiting for something to begin. Waiting! Waiting! Waiting! Well, my plane's on the runway, my seat belt is fastened and I'm ready to take off.

MITCHELL. And this time you're going first class.

PAUL. (*Trying to get loose—frightened.*) Goddamn it, you really got me tied up here.

MITCHELL. That's the name of the game.

PAUL. Arlene, look in my left pocket.

ARLENE. Why?

PAUL. Just look. What have you got to lose?

ARLENE. (*Reaches into his pocket and takes out a small gift wrapped box.*) Oh, Paul, you shouldn't have. I didn't get you anything for Christmas. I didn't think I'd have to. (*She sits down on nearby chair and unwraps the gift.*)

PAUL. I didn't have time to buy a card. (*To* MITCHELL.) How late are the stores open?

MITCHELL. 'Til nine o'clock, but I don't think you're going to make it. (PAUL *manages to move himself and chair next to* ARLENE.)

ARLENE. (*Taking a watch out of the box. Disappointed.*) Another watch! He bought me another watch. (*Reprimanding.*) Paul, do you take pleasure in tormenting me?

PAUL. That's a digital. You don't have one like that.

ARLENE. I don't want this watch. (*Puts it back in box.*) You take it back where you bought it.

MITCHELL. How can he take it back? Let me see that. (*Takes the box from her and looks at the watch.*) Not bad. How much did you pay for this?

PAUL. A hundred bucks.

MITCHELL. Bullshit! It's a Timex.

PAUL. You want to buy it? I'll take fifty.

MITCHELL. I'll give you twenty.

ARLENE. (*To* MITCHELL.) Why do you want a lady's watch?

MITCHELL. It's for my mother. I like to buy her things.

PAUL. For your mother? What a baby! He's a baby. Little baby . . .

MITCHELL. We'll see who's a baby. (*Takes a hypodermic needle from his bag.*) Ahhh, here it is. (*Squirts out some of the liquid into the air.*)

PAUL. (*With growing concern.*) What the hell's that?

MITCHELL. Novocaine. I give you a shot in both arms. I give you a shot in both legs, and before you know it you're a ball of rubber and all we have to do is bounce you into the bathroom.

ARLENE. Your only hope is to hold your breath in the bathtub and try to stay afloat, but how long can anyone do that?

PAUL. Arlene, get your coat. We're going home.

ARLENE. If you could only let me go. Give me a divorce.

PAUL. Never!

MITCHELL. (*Studying* PAUL.) We have a problem here. You're going to have to take off your jacket and roll up your sleeves.

PAUL. Oh, yeah? And who do you think I am, Houdini?

MITCHELL. Let's see if I can work something out here.

(*While holding the needle in one hand, he proceeds to push* PAUL'S *jacket off his shoulders and unbutton his shirt so that he can expose his arm for the needle.*)

PAUL. It's the insurance, isn't it?

MITCHELL. What insurance?

PAUL. My life insurance. That's the real reason you're killing me. Now it makes sense. I knew it had nothing to do with love.

ARLENE. Paul, Mitchell doesn't need your money.

MITCHELL. Well, how much is it, exactly?

PAUL. Two hundred thousand dollars. (MITCHELL *whistles. He's impressed.*)

ARLENE. Paul, I thought you only had fifty thousand.

PAUL. Well, last month I thought it over and I didn't think it would be enough.

ARLENE. Paul Miller, you're a good man.

PAUL. And that's only the beginning. If I die in a plane crash, it's double.

MITCHELL. Well, we can't get a plane in here, so let's get on with it.

PAUL. (*To* ARLENE.) You had a good thing being married to me. I don't care how you felt about it. The trouble with people like you is that you're never satisfied. Don't you realize nobody has it perfect. Look at that wedding band you're wearing. I remember you wouldn't even get married unless I got you that ring. You wanted everyone to know that you were Mrs. Paul Miller. That you belonged to me. That I belonged to you. That I owned you and that you owned me. That we owned each other. (*To* MITCHELL.) And you, Doctor Lovell. You'll live to regret not remaining single. If I can't make my marriage work, what chance have you got?

MITCHELL. Love conquers all.

PAUL. Love conquers shit! Arlene, if you wanted to have an affair, all you had to do was come to me and ask me. I would have said "no" and that would have been the end of it.

MITCHELL. (*To* ARLENE.) Help me get his pant legs up. (*As* MITCHELL *and* ARLENE *roll up* PAUL'S *pants, they discover he's wearing garters.*) Garters! Who wears garters! Now that tells you something about the man.

PAUL. So help me God, if you go through with this I'll come back and haunt you from the grave. (*Makes weird whistling sounds.*)

ARLENE. (*A little suspicious.*) What do you think, Mitchell?

MITCHELL. He's just bluffing.

PAUL. You want my personal opinion of this whole thing?

MITCHELL. Sure.

ARLENE. Yes.

PAUL. (*Yelling.*) Help!

MITCHELL. Are you crazy? You're gonna bring everybody up here.

PAUL. Help!

ARLENE. What's the matter with you, Paul?

PAUL. Help!

MITCHELL. Quick! Bring me a washcloth.

ARLENE. What for?

MITCHELL. I want to gag him.

ARLENE. Right.

PAUL. Help! Help!

MITCHELL. Hurry! (ARLENE *rushes to the bathroom.* MITCHELL *puts his hand over* PAUL'S *mouth to quiet him.*)

PAUL. Help!

MITCHELL. Will you stop that! (PAUL *bites his hand.*) Owwww! (*Pulls back in pain.*) Son of a bitch bit me.

PAUL. Help!

ARLENE. (*Rushes out with the washcloth.*) Quiet, Paul! (*Hands towel to* MITCHELL.) Here. (MITCHELL *takes the washcloth and hands her the needle.*) Here. (*He starts shoving washcloth into* PAUL'S *mouth.*)

PAUL. Help!

ARLENE. (*To* MITCHELL.) I can't get over how clean the bathrooms are here. I wouldn't mind coming back again. (PAUL *stops shouting.*)

MITCHELL. There!

ARLENE. (*Impressed.*) That's very good. I didn't think that would work.

MITCHELL. (*Backs up to admire his work and accidentally backs into needle that* ARLENE *is holding.*) Owwww!

ARLENE. I'm really sorry. Thank God you weren't facing me.

MITCHELL. Forget the novocaine. Let's get this over with.

ARLENE. (*Looking at* PAUL *who seems to be sinking fast.*) Mitchell, would you mind very much if I said goodbye to him first?

MITCHELL. No, just hurry it up. (*He goes into bathroom.*)

ARLENE. (*Walking around* PAUL. *She tries to be very tactful.* PAUL *winks at her furiously, trying to get her to free him.*) You know, Paul, there are things in life that are very difficult to justify. You haven't been a bad husband. I'll bet a lot of women would have traded places with me. Unfortunately for you, you were the wrong guy at the wrong place with the wrong woman. I'd hate to have you go out thinking this is all your fault. Is it so wrong for a person to put her personal needs ahead of everyone else's? (PAUL *shakes his head.*) You're probably right, but everybody's doing it. I'd give anything not to have to go through with this. Anything. If only you weren't so possessive. If only you weren't so in love with me. If only you would give me a divorce. How about it, Paul? (PAUL *shakes his head furiously indicating that he won't. He tries to move himself and the chair toward the door.*) I've got to hand it to you, Paul. You're a "one woman man."

MITCHELL. (*Coming out of the bathroom. He's limping as a result of the novocaine in his rear.*) Let's get this over with. Okay, Paul. It's time for your bath. (*The two drag* PAUL *in the chair, into the bathroom.*)

ARLENE. Do you think we should add some hot water? He hates a cold tub.

MITCHELL. What's the difference? I hate this kind of work. (*They're now in the bathroom. There's a beat followed by a loud splash. A moment later,* ARLENE *comes out followed by* MITCHELL.) Are you all right?

ARLENE. I think so. Is he dead?

MITCHELL. (*Glancing back into bathroom.*) I guess so. He's kind of blue. Let's get out of here.

(*They go about gathering their things quietly. We hear the faint sound of Christmas music.* MITCHELL *gets his coat and his doctor's bag.* ARLENE *gets her coat and her shopping bag. The two manage not to look at one another until they get to the front door.* MITCHELL *unlocks the door.* ARLENE *looks at him.*)

ARLENE. Merry Christmas, Mitchell.

MITCHELL. (*Opens door.*) You'd better drive. My ass is asleep.

(MITCHELL *turns off the lights and shuts the door behind them. There is a beat. Suddenly* PAUL *comes staggering out of the bathroom. The chair is still attached to him. He has the shower curtain wrapped around him and is soaking wet. The gag is gone from his mouth.)*

PAUL. That's it. Tomorrow morning we're seeing a marriage counselor. (*He slumps down in chair as the Christmas music swells. The CURTAIN COMES DOWN.*)

END OF SCENE 1

ACT ONE

SCENE 2

Room 907, the same Howard Johnson hotel. The room is identical except for different color drapes and a different color bedspread. The floor lamp has been replaced by a low, round table. It is the 4th of July, six months later. Early evening. There is a red, white and blue bunting on the headboard, replacing the Christmas wreath. In the background we hear patriotic march music.

AT RISE: ARLENE *is pacing back and forth, nervously. She goes to her handbag and takes out a vial of pills and goes to the phone. The march music fades out.* ARLENE *dials the phone.*

ARLENE. (*On phone.*) Hello, Mitchell. This is Arlene. Don't ask questions. I'm at the Howard Johnson's, room 907. Hear this? (*She shakes the pills into the mouthpiece.*) These are sleeping pills. I just want you to know I'm killing myself. (*She hangs up. There is furious knocking at the door.*)

PAUL. (*Offstage.*) Arlene! Arlene! You didn't do it yet, did you?

(ARLENE *opens the door and lets* PAUL *in. He is wearing a grey summer suit, white shirt, black shoes and a striped grey tie with a touch of color. He is carrying a paper bag.*)

ARLENE. Hello, Paul.

PAUL. (*Still standing at the door.*) I would have been here sooner but I got caught in the mob out there waiting for the fireworks to start. (*Looks around.*) Are you alone?

ARLENE. Yes.

PAUL. Are you sure? (*He peeks around the door.*)

ARLENE. Yes, I'm killing myself. I'm not throwing a party.

PAUL. (*Enters and closes the door.*) Why are you killing yourself? If it's about the divorce, my lawyer's working on it. He's slow. What can I tell you? I'm trying to work it out so that you get everything.

ARLENE. I'd rather not talk about it. I just wanted you to be the last person on earth to see me alive.

PAUL. That's very thoughtful. (PAUL *starts to empty contents of the bag onto the round table. It's a bucket of Kentucky Fried Chicken and a six-pack of beer.*) I got you some chicken and beer. I thought it might cheer you up.

ARLENE. That's a very nice tie.

PAUL. (*Standing and admiring his own tie.*) Yeah, I'm into colors now.

ARLENE. Very becoming. (*She sits down at the table.*)

PAUL. Yeah, I thought so too. I bought five others just like it.

ARLENE. (*Picking up a piece of chicken.*) You remembered. Extra crispy.

PAUL. (*Takes off his jacket and sits down.*) I missed you, Arlene. It's been a long time.

ARLENE. Yes, it has. Almost six months.

PAUL. Six months, thirteen days and twenty-three hours.

ARLENE. (*Looking through bucket of chicken.*) They gave you all wings.

PAUL. Everyone in this world shafts you. I wanted breasts.

ARLENE. (*Rises.*) Paul, do you still love me?

PAUL. How's that?

ARLENE. Do you still love me? I would like to go out knowing someone still loves me..

PAUL. (*Rises.*) Do I still love you? Do I still love you? Arlene, that's my life loving you. I never stopped loving you. (*Goes to bathroom door and quickly opens it and looks in. He does the same with the closet door.*) Even last December when you drowned me, I never stopped loving you.

ARLENE. Poor Paul. How I must have hurt you. (*She grabs her pills, leaps over the bed and rushes for the window.*) I'm a rotten person. I deserve to die.

PAUL. (*Rushes to her and pulls her away from the window.*) No, no, Arlene. (*He embraces her.*)

ARLENE. Do you want to know my plan? I'm going to take a bottle of sleeping pills, sit on the window sill and stab myself.

PAUL. That's a good plan. That would work. (*He takes the pills from her, looks at vial and puts them in his pants pocket.*)

ARLENE. I didn't want to take any chances. (*They both go back to the table and resume eating.*) Oh, Paul, isn't life strange the way it takes so many twists and turns? It's like a roller coaster. You're up, you're down, you veer to the right, you veer to the left, you hope to God you don't fall out . . .

PAUL. Hey, that's what I'm studying in school.

ARLENE. You're going to school?

PAUL. Two nights a week. I know one of the reasons you left me was because you thought I was shallow. (*Rises.*) I'm not shallow anymore, Arlene. You know what I'm doing? I'm taking a self-realization course.

ARLENE. I'm very impressed.

PAUL. I've got a terrific teacher. You should meet him. You'd love him. His name is Malcolm Dewey. He's only twenty-five years old and very short, but he seems to know everything. You'd never kill yourself if you met Malcolm Dewey. (*Sits.*) I swear, Arlene, I'm now able to grasp the meaning of life and in only one month.

ARLENE. That must be so encouraging.

PAUL. He sums up his whole philosophy in two words. "Me first!" "If you're good to yourself you're good to the world." A truly healthy, selfish person would never commit suicide. Repeat after me. A truly healthy, selfish person would never commit suicide.

ARLENE and PAUL. A truly healthy, selfish person would never commit suicide.

ARLENE. There's no cole slaw.

PAUL. Another shaft. Next week we go on to physical awareness. He actually gets you to talk to parts of your body. It's great for lonely people. (*To hands.*) Hello hands. How are you? Hellow elbow. Hello knees . . .

ARLENE. That's . . . fascinating. They didn't give you any napkins.

PAUL. Another shaft.

ARLENE. (*Rises.*) I've got Kleenex.

PAUL. (*Rises and follows her.*) I'm a changed man, Arlene. I even stopped drinking.

ARLENE. I didn't know you started. (*She gets Kleenex from her handbag.* PAUL *takes one and the two of them begin wiping each other's mouth.*)

PAUL. Yeah, for a while I was going through a case of beer a day, trying to forget you.

ARLENE. It's a wonder you didn't put on any weight.

PAUL. I cut out potatoes.

ARLENE. You love potatoes.

PAUL. Yes, but potatoes don't help you forget . . . So, it's over. So it's over between you and the dentist . . . It's over.

ARLENE. I haven't told you everything.

PAUL. No kidding. He hurt you, right? Let me see the bruises.

ARLENE. No, no. Nothing like that.

PAUL. Did he force you to do things? What kind of monster is he? Did he make you do housework? Was it another woman? (ARLENE *cries.*) Another woman. What's wrong with that guy? Why can't people be happy with what they got? I knew it. Any man with unlimited use of novocaine . . . Okay, whose wife was it this time?

ARLENE. It was horrible. The other day I was out shopping. I thought I'd surprise him at work.

PAUL. Yes.

ARLENE. (*Acting it out.*) I walked in. There was no one there. I couldn't hear a sound. So I tiptoed into his office. I opened the door . . .

PAUL. Yes.

ARLENE. And there they were, in the chair.

PAUL. In the chair!!!?

ARLENE. He and his dental assistant.

PAUL. With Judy? I thought she just cleaned teeth . . . Scum! Scum of the earth.

ARLENE. She sure is.

PAUL. I'm talking about him.

ARLENE. He ruined my life, Paul, not to mention yours. He provoked my fantasies. He blinded me. He hypnotized me. He lured me. He seduced me.

PAUL. When I think of his hands in my mouth . . .

ARLENE. He actually tricked me into falling in love with him. He made a mockery of our marriage. He betrayed you as a patient. He betrayed me as a mistress.

PAUL. There's no loyalty in the world. (*Looking through bucket of chicken.*) No honor in the world. No fidelity. There's nothing. Nobody gives a shit anymore. (*Indicates chicken.*) I wanted breasts. They gave me wings. The world sucks! Don't kill yourself, Arlene. You're killing the wrong person. He's the one who deserves to die. (*Caught up in it.*) People like him should be destroyed. I'll kill him! I'll kill him! I'll rip him to shreds. I'll burn him. I'll blow him up. I'll stab him. I'll boil him . . .

ARLENE. (*Taking a pistol out of her handbag and handing it to* PAUL.) We don't have much time. Here's a gun.

PAUL. A gun! What am I going to do with a gun?

ARLENE. You're going to kill him, Paul.

PAUL. You want me to kill Dr. Lovell? Aren't you overreacting? Where did you get a gun?

ARLENE. At Sears. It's their own brand.

PAUL. A Kenmore?!!!

ARLENE. Do you know how to use a gun?

PAUL. Sure. Nothing to it. You aim it, you pull the trigger and five days later you're back on the street again.

ARLENE. He should be here any minute.

PAUL. He's coming here? (*Goes to door and looks through the peep hole.*)

ARLENE. I hate him. I wanted him to find my body. I wanted to ruin his day. Oh, Paul. It'll be wonderful from now on. Just you and me again.

PAUL. Arlene, if it's just you and me, why do I have to kill him?

ARLENE. Don't you see, Paul, my hatred for him is so deep that as long as he's alive I'll never be able to give you a hundred percent in bed.

PAUL. Who needs a hundred percent? (*There's a knock at the door.*)

MITCHELL. (*Offstage, excitedly.*) Arlene! Arlene! Don't do it! (*Frantic knocking continues.*)

ARLENE. That's him.

PAUL. (*Pointing the gun at the door.*) Good. Open the door and I'll shoot him in self defense.

ARLENE. No, no. You hide in the closet. (*She gives* PAUL *the chicken, beer, and his jacket and starts leading him towards closet.*) I'll get him over to the bed. The minute we start making love, you jump out of the closet and shoot him.

PAUL. Arlene, why can't I shoot him before you start making love?

ARLENE. I want to humiliate him the way he humiliated me. I want him to suffer.

PAUL. Oh, this is going to be good.

MITCHELL. (*Offstage, still knocking at the door.*) Arlene! Arlene! Am I too late?

ARLENE. (*To* PAUL.) I love you. (*She pushes him into the closet and starts towards front door. The closet door opens and* PAUL *sticks his head out.*)

PAUL. Arlene, I love you. (ARLENE *motions for* PAUL *to get back in the closet. He does. She turns off the overhead light. The closet door opens again and* PAUL *sticks his head out.*) This is the best Fourth of July I ever had.

ARLENE. (*Motioning for him to go back into the closet. Stage whisper.*) And it's not over yet.

(PAUL *is back in the closet as* ARLENE *opens the door.* MITCHELL *enters. He has a long slim bag with a bottle of wine in it.*)

MITCHELL. Arlene. I'm glad I got here in time. I drove through red lights, I drove through stop signs, I drove through railroad crossings. Thank God, I'm a doctor. I'm allowed to drive like a maniac. (ARLENE *closes the door.*) Arlene, what I did was inexcusable. I never felt so low in my life. These past few days without you have been just awful.

ARLENE. They were worse for me, Mitchell.

MITCHELL. Actually, they were worse for Judy. She's in the hospital.

ARLENE. Isn't that terrible. Why?

MITCHELL. When you went screaming out of the office, I jumped up from the chair. I hit the wrong button, the chair folded in half and Judy's in traction.

ARLENE. Poor Judy. I should send her flowers.

MITCHELL. Me too. (*Hands her wine.*) Oh, by the way, I brought your favorite.

ARLENE. (*Takes the wine out of bag.*) Blue Nun. You're too good to me.

MITCHELL. I didn't know whether you'd still be alive.

(*Sniffs.*) I smell chicken and beer in here. (*Walks around room sniffing.*)

ARLENE. It's the Fourth of July. It's in the air.

MITCHELL. (*Outside closet door.*) I'll bet every jerk in town bought chicken and beer today.

(MITCHELL'S *back is to the closet.* PAUL *comes out of the closet, angry.* ARLENE *waves him back in.*)

ARLENE. (*Embracing* MITCHELL.) Oh, Mitchell, I came so close to death, but now that I see you I realize that killing myself was the wrong thing to do.

MITCHELL. There's got to be another way.

ARLENE. Of course there is. I can't blame Judy for wanting you. It must be unbearable to have to work for someone as irresistible as you.

MITCHELL. You're very perceptive.

ARLENE. I missed you, Mitchell. Give me one of those dirty kisses you're so famous for.

MITCHELL. If that's what you want. (*They kiss.* MITCHELL'S *back is to the closet.* PAUL *comes out of the closet, gun in one hand, a piece of chicken that he's eating in the other. He motions to* ARLENE *to get* MITCHELL *into bed so that he can kill him.* ARLENE *waves him back to the closet.* PAUL *goes back in and closes the door. Coming out of kiss, he starts removing his pants.*) Arlene, I take my hat off to you. When I came up here I didn't know what to expect. I thought if you were alive, there would be a lot of screaming and yelling and carrying on.

ARLENE. That's not my style.

MITCHELL. You've turned a negative situation into something positive and beautiful. (*He goes toward closet with his clothing.*) By the way, what made you pick this place? This is where we tried to kill Schumcko.

ARLENE. (*Heading* MITCHELL *off at the closet. She takes his clothes.*) Forget about Schmucko. You go warm up the bed.

(MITCHELL *goes to the bed.* ARLENE *opens the closet door and throws his clothes in at* PAUL. *Closes door again.*)

MITCHELL. You know what we're going to do? You and I are going on a Carribbean cruise. Seven days and seven nights and we're not coming out of the cabin once.

ARLENE. I can't wait. (*She gets on the bed with* MITCHELL.)

MITCHELL. (*Embracing her.*) Arlene, this is the best Fourth of July I ever had.

ARLENE. And it's not over yet. (MITCHELL *begins kissing her passionately. Yelling towards closet.*) Now! Now!

MITCHELL. What's the rush?

(*Continues kissing* ARLENE. *The closet door opens and* PAUL *comes out, gun, bucket of chicken and beer in hand. He tiptoes over to table and sets down the chicken and beer. He tiptoes to wall switch and turns on more lights. Then he tiptoes to the front of the bed and stands there pointing the gun at* MITCHELL.)

PAUL. Schmucko's here!

MITCHELL. (*Startled, and still holding* ARLENE *looks up.*) Paul!!! Look, Arlene, it's Paul.

PAUL. Okay, lover boy. Hands off and up.

MITCHELL. Paul, you missed your check-up last month.

ARLENE. Shoot him! Shoot him, Paul!

MITCHELL. Arlene! What are you saying?

ARLENE. Shoot! Shoot! (*She breaks away from* MITCHELL *and jumps off bed.*)

MITCHELL. Come on, Arlene. He's got a gun. (*He runs behind* ARLENE, *holds her and uses her as a shield. To* PAUL.) Is that thing loaded?

ARLENE. You bet. Shoot! Shoot!

PAUL. I can't. Move away. (ARLENE *tries moving away.* MITCHELL *holds on to her.*)

MITCHELL. I'll tell you what. Free office visits for a whole year.

ARLENE. Shoot him, Paul! Shoot him!

MITCHELL. Why, Arlene? Why? We just kissed and made up.

ARLENE. I'm getting even with you, Mitchell. (*She kicks* MITCHELL *in the leg, breaks free and runs to* PAUL's *side.*)

MITCHELL. Owww!

PAUL. That's right, Lovell. Nobody cheats on my wife.

MITCHELL. (*Grabbing pillows to protect himself and jumping on bed.*) Don't shoot, Paul! Please don't shoot!

PAUL. What a baby! Little baby! Baby, baby . . .

ARLENE. Come on, Paul, shoot!

MITCHELL. You'll never get away with this.

ARLENE. Yes you will.

MITCHELL. No, he won't.

ARLENE. It doesn't matter.

PAUL. What do you mean, it doesn't matter?

ARLENE. Never mind. Just shoot.

MITCHELL. You'll get the chair, Paul.

ARLENE. I'll get you a lawyer, Paul.

MITCHELL. He'll take all your money, Paul.

ARLENE. Shoot him!

MITCHELL. Don't shoot him!

ARLENE. Shoot him!

MITCHELL. Don't shoot him!

PAUL. (*Confused. Holding his head.*) Wait! Stop it! Both of you. My head. You're making me crazy. (MITCHELL *jumps off the bed and runs into the closet, closing the door behind him.*)

ARLENE. Get him, Paul.

PAUL. (*Goes to the closet and pulls on it. He can't open it.*) Get out of there! (PAUL *stands to the side of the door and starts coughing.*) Fire! Fire! (*Coughs some more. The closet door opens and* MITCHELL *starts running toward the front door. Halfway there he stops, realizing he's been duped.* PAUL, *ordering* MITCHELL *all over the room with the gun.*) All right, smart guy. Over here! Over there! Over there! Over here! Arlene, get his pants.

ARLENE. (*Going to closet to get* MITCHELL'S *pants.*) Why aren't you shooting him?

PAUL. There's a better way to get rid of this bum.

ARLENE. Like what?

PAUL. Suicide.

MITCHELL. Why would you want to kill yourself?

PAUL. *Your* suicide.

ARLENE. Why didn't I think of that?

PAUL. Why should we get blamed for it? We're going to push him out the window. They'll think he jumped. Then you and I get the chicken, the beer, the Blue Nun and go home and live happily ever after. (*He kisses* ARLENE *on the cheek.*)

MITCHELL. Why would I commit suicide? I've got a good practice, I'm out of the stock market, I just took up tennis, I've got all my hair . . .

PAUL. (*To* MITCHELL.) Over by the window.

ARLENE. Wait, Paul. There's one thing missing.

PAUL. What's that?

ARLENE. A suicide note.

PAUL. Good girl. We'll be a team yet. (*To* MITCHELL.) Sit down. Arlene, get some paper. (MITCHELL *sits at the table.*)

ARLENE. (*Reaches into drawer and pulls out postcard.*) There's no paper. Just a couple of postcards.

PAUL. So he'll write small.

ARLENE. (*Looking at card.*) Look how beautiful they make this hotel look. There are no trees out front.

PAUL. Everybody shafts you. (*To* MITCHELL.) Now take the pen and start writing. (*Points gun to his own temple.*) Let's think about this. How do we start?

ARLENE. To whom it may concern.

PAUL. Good girl. (*To* MITCHELL.) To whom it may concern . . .

ARLENE. Good beginning.

PAUL. (*Dictating.*) I, Mitchell Lovell, being of sound mind . . .

ARLENE. . . . and body . . .

PAUL. (*Gives* ARLENE *a quick look and then continues dictating.*) Have decided to . . .

ARLENE. . . . kill myself!

PAUL. Isn't it wonderful, Arlene? We're doing things together again.

ARLENE. Keep it moving, Paul.

PAUL. Right. (*Dictating.*) Life is cruel and I'm not too thrilled with the government either. (MITCHELL *and* ARLENE *look at* PAUL.) That's to throw them off the track.

ARLENE. Now. Sign it, Mitchell Lovell, D.D.S.

PAUL. (*To* ARLENE *lovingly.*) We're back together again, aren't we?

MITCHELL. There's only room for one "D."

PAUL. That's all you deserve. Well, Dr. Lovell, what do you think?

MITCHELL. Here's what I think. (*He rips up the postcard and throws it in the air.*)

ARLENE. We don't have time for games, Mitchell.

PAUL. (*To* ARLENE.) Get another postcard.

MITCHELL. No!

PAUL. What do you mean, no?

MITCHELL. No, I'm not writing any more notes and no, I'm not committing suicide. If you want to kill me you'll have to pull that trigger yourself.

ARLENE. Pull the trigger! Pull the trigger.

MITCHELL. I'll be dead and you'll go to jail for life.

ARLENE. Plug him.

MITCHELL. By the time you get out of prison, Arlene will be in her nineties. Try and make that marriage exciting.

PAUL. You're not gonna jump?

MITCHELL. No.

PAUL. Will you at least stand by the window so we can push you?

MITCHELL. No. If you want me dead you'll have to pull the trigger yourself. Go ahead. (*He defiantly backs* PAUL *away.*) Go ahead, shoot.

PAUL. Shoot?

MITCHELL. Shoot!

PAUL. (*Thinking.*) Shoot!

MITCHELL. (*To* ARLENE.) Arlene, your wanting to kill me is the best thing that ever happened to me. To hate me so much, that's what I call real love.

ARLENE. I hate you.

MITCHELL. You love me.

PAUL. *I* hate you.

MITCHELL. You're not in this. (*He pushes* PAUL *aside and goes to* ARLENE.) Arlene, I'm glad Paul has a gun. I could leave if I wanted to. I could run right out of here. But I won't. I want to stay right here with you because I love you, Arlene.

(*During the following,* PAUL *sits down. He's confused as to what to do next.*)

ARLENE. (*Coldly, pacing around the room.*) Go on.

MITCHELL. You were right about me. I know I'm immature. I know I have difficulties making a commitment. To tell you the truth I was frightened when you moved in with me. I've been a bachelor too many years.

ARLENE. Keep going.

MITCHELL. Judy doesn't mean anything to me. She never did. It was always you. Paul was right, I am a baby.

ARLENE. Go on.

MITCHELL. I love you, Arlene. I loved you from the very first moment you walked into my office with Paul. I loved you through all the sneaking around we had to do. Through all the deceiving and the cheating we had to do, I knew you were something special.

ARLENE. If only I could believe you.

MITCHELL. How can I prove it? (*To* PAUL.) Paul, do you think I'm lying?

PAUL. (*Still sitting in chair.*) I'm the wrong guy to ask.

MITCHELL. Arlene, you want me to shout it to the world? I'll shout it to the world.

ARLENE. Shout it.

MITCHELL. (*Opening window and shouting.*) Hey, world. I love Mrs. Paul Miller.

ARLENE. Paul, did you hear that? He really means it. I don't know about you but I feel very small right now. I think we owe Doctor Lovell an apology.

MITCHELL. (*Going to* ARLENE.) I love you, Arlene. I love you! I love you! I love you! (*He kisses* ARLENE. *She lifts one leg.*)

PAUL. (*Rising and going to* ARLENE.) And I love you, I love you, I love you. (*He kisses her and lifts one leg.*)

ARLENE. When it rains, it pours.

PAUL. Okay, Arlene. Choose between us, him . . . (*Pointing gun at* MITCHELL.) or me. (*Points gun at himself.*)

MITCHELL. (*Getting down on one knee.*) I'll never cheat on you again. Tomorrow I'm firing Judy.

ARLENE. You don't have to go that far.

MITCHELL. Just as well. She's been hinting for a raise anyway. I love you, Arlene. I love you, I love you, I love you.

PAUL. (*Sits on* MITCHELL'S *knee and points the gun at him.*) You say you love her, you love her, you love her? (*Rises and goes to* ARLENE.) Let's see how much you love her. (*He grabs* ARLENE *and puts the gun to her head.*) Either you jump or she gets it.

ARLENE. Paul, I think you just stepped over the line of good taste.

MITCHELL. Are you nuts? Are you out of your mind? Where's your sense of decency?

PAUL. Decency! Decency! I'm trying to hold on to a marriage. Jump!

MITCHELL. (*Moves toward Upstage Right window.*) Come on. There's cement down there.

PAUL. Good. It'll break your fall. Now jump.

MITCHELL. Paul, have a heart.

PAUL. I'm counting to three. One . . .

MITCHELL. Don't shoot her. I'll jump.

ARLENE. No, Mitchell, no!

PAUL. Two!

MITCHELL. Okay! Okay! I said I'd jump. What's the rush?

PAUL. The rush is, the sooner you hit the ground, the sooner Arlene and I can start rebuilding this marriage of ours. Jump!

MITCHELL. You'll never be able to give her what she needs.

PAUL. (*To* ARLENE.) What do you need? I'll buy it for you.

MITCHELL. She needs understanding. She needs compassion. She needs warmth, empathy, touching, feeling . . .

PAUL. She'll learn to live with less. Now jump!

ARLENE. Mitchell, I swear I never meant for things to go this far.

PAUL. I said, jump!

MITCHELL. I'm going. I only ask one thing of you, Arlene.

ARLENE. (*Enthralled.*) Sure, anything.

MITCHELL. One last kiss.

ARLENE. Can I, Paul?

PAUL. You're not kissing anybody. No kissing.

ARLENE. Oh, come on, Paul. Have a heart. One innocent kiss. A man is about to die.

MITCHELL. It's not like I'm asking for the works.

PAUL. Jump!

(MITCHELL *climbs onto the window, sits on the window ledge with his feet dangling out of sight. The window is large enough so that his head clears it.*)

MITCHELL. All right! I'll see you, Arlene. Boy, we sure had some good times.

PAUL. Jump! (MITCHELL *pushes himself off and disappears.* ARLENE *screams.* PAUL, *his back to window. He is still pointing the gun at* ARLENE.) Jump! Jump! (*To* ARLENE.) What are you screaming about? Jump! (*Turns, shocked.*) Oh, my God he did it! Who asked him to jump? I didn't think he'd do it. Why did he do it? He shouldn't have done it. (*He realizes he has the gun in his hand and suddenly wants no part of it and flings it out the window.*) I'm fed up with this whole thing. (*Sits on bed. We hear a gunshot down below. Suddenly* MITCHELL *pops up outside the window.*)

MITCHELL. You just killed a dog.

ARLENE. Look! It's a miracle.

PAUL. (*Looking out the other window.*) There's a goddamn ledge out there.

MITCHELL. Of course there's a ledge. You think I'm a putz like you?

PAUL. (*Angrily goes towards* MITCHELL.) All right. Stop clowning around. Jump!

MITCHELL. No!

PAUL. Jump!

MITCHELL. No!

PAUL. (*Grabs pillow and starts out the window after him.*) All right, I warned you.

ARLENE. Paul, that's dangerous.

PAUL. I'll push him off with my bare hands. (PAUL *starts chasing* MITCHELL *on the ledge toward Stage Left.*) Jump!

MITCHELL. Up yours!

ARLENE. Run, Mitchell! Run! (MITCHELL *appears at Stage Left window, which is closed. He knocks on window.*)

MITCHELL. (*Shouting.*) Let me in! (ARLENE *runs to the closed window and tries to open it. It's too late.* PAUL *is on top of him hitting him over the head with the pillow.*)

PAUL. Jump!

MITCHELL. (*Shouting to* ARLENE.) I'll be back! (MITCHELL *goes Off Stage Left with* PAUL *pursuing him.*)

PAUL. Jump!

MITCHELL. (*Offstage.*) No! (*They both disappear Offstage.*)

ARLENE. (*Looking down toward street.*) Oh, my God. Everybody's looking up here. (*Suddenly* MITCHELL *appears at the window heading towards Stage Right obviously still being pursued by* PAUL.)

MITCHELL. (*Knocks at window; shouting.*) Arlene, open up!

ARLENE. (*Loudly.*) How did you get past Paul?

MITCHELL. I have no idea. Let me in. (ARLENE *starts to open the window but it's too late.* PAUL *is next to* MITCHELL, *hitting him with the pillow.*)

ARLENE. (*To* MITCHELL.) Come to the other window. (ARLENE *rushes to the open window.* MITCHELL, *still pursued by* PAUL, *has not time to come inside.*)

PAUL. (*Shouting.*) Jump!

MITCHELL. I'm getting dizzy! (*They disappear Stage Right.*)

ARLENE. (*Calling after* MITCHELL.) Don't look down!

PAUL. (*Offstage.*) Look down!

ARLENE. (*Calling to them.*) Mitchell! Paul! Be careful! (*Suddenly we hear the sound of fireworks in the distance.* ARLENE *notices lights in the sky.*) Oh, fireworks! I love fireworks. I love the Fourth of July. (*She goes to wall switch and shuts off the overhead lights. She walks around the room almost in a daze.*) It's a wonderful holiday. It reminds me of being young again. When things were so simple and innocent. I didn't know what a man was until I was twelve. Now, I'm almost forty and I have two men on a ledge risking their lives for me. Which one do I choose? Which one do I hurt? Which one do I love forever and which one do I destroy? I don't know what to do anymore. I'm so confused. What do I want? What do I really want? I've got to get out of here. I've got to get help. (*She grabs her handbag and opens the front door.*) Life is so complicated for those of us who think. (*She exits.*)

MITCHELL. (*Offstage, shouting.*) Arlene! What room are we in? They all look alike. (*He appears at the Stage Left window and crawls in and immediately falls to the floor, very nervous, very frightened, out of breath.*) Oh, God, the floor. I love the floor. It was awful. All those people down there shouting at me to jump. I went all around the building. They do very well here. Every single room is rented. (*Looks around.*) Arlene! Arlene! (*Gets up and looks in the bathroom.*) Arlene! Where the hell did she go? (*He slips on his shoes, grabs his jacket and goes to the front door.*) I can't help but feel I'm forgetting something. (*He spots the bottle of Blue Nun, picks it up, opens the door, stops, realizes something and runs to the window.*) Paul! Paul! (*He looks out the window.*) My God, he must have fallen. (*He exits quickly, slamming the door behind him. There is a beat.*)

PAUL. (*Offstage, faintly.*) Help! Help! (*He suddenly appears, Stage Left, with his back to the window and his arms outstretched.*) Help! Help! (*With his back to the window he swivels into the room and, unable to stop, swivels out again.*) Help! Help! (*He swivels in again, this time able to stop. He gets off the window sill and steps onto the dresser. With his arms still outstretched, he looks down at the floor as if it were nine stories down.*) Help! Help! (*He tries to step down but is afraid to. He bends down and picks up a hairbrush from the dresser and, by way of testing the distance from the dresser to the floor, lets the hairbrush fall. Satisfied that the floor isn't too far down, he manages to step down on the floor. With his arms still outstretched, he walks towards the bathroom, as if still on the ledge, still afraid to fall.*) I saw death. It winked at me. (*He opens the door to the bathroom and looks in.*) Arlene! Arlene! (*With arms still outstretched he opens the closet door.*) Doctor Lovell! (*He starts to go towards a chair. He notices something on the upper sleeve of his shirt. He brushes it.*) A pigeon shit on me! . . . I can't take this anymore. (*He sits down on the chair with his arms still outstretched. He stares blankly ahead for a few beats. He then reaches into his pants pocket and pulls out* ARLENE'S *vial of sleeping pills. He looks at it, opens it, empties all the pills in his hand and slowly lifts them towards his mouth. Inches from his mouth, he stops and stares at his hand.*) Hello, hand! (*He turns his hand over, dropping all the pills to the floor.*) Hello, arm. Hello, elbow. (*Looks down at his knees.*) Hello, knees. (*The CURTAIN STARTS TO FALL.*) Guess what, fellas. We've been shafted again.

END OF ACT ONE

ACT TWO

PLACE: *Room 1015. The same Howard Johnson hotel. The room is practically the same except for different drapes and bedspread. Over the headboard is a "Happy New Year" sign. The table and armchairs are no longer there. In their place is a wooden platform base approximately three feet wide and five feet long and about ten inches high. The cover to the platform leans against the nearby wall. There is a bottle of champagne and two glasses on the dresser.*

TIME: *New Year's Eve. Six months later. Late evening.*

AT RISE: MITCHELL, *in tuxedo pants, shirt and bow tie is on the floor putting the last few nails into the platform base. After several beats,* PAUL *enters from the bathroom, wiping his hands on a towel. He is wearing an old-fashioned, tight-fitting tuxedo.*

PAUL. You know, I've got six towels from this place already. How are you doing?

MITCHELL. I'm almost finished. Next time we do this, remember to bring two hammers.

PAUL. If we do this right, there won't be a next time.

MITCHELL. (*Continuing to hammer.*) You know, this is the first New Year's Eve in my life I don't have a date.

PAUL. I hate New Year's Eve. I never liked wearing a tuxedo. (*Looks in imaginary mirror Downstage. He drapes the towel over his left arm.*) Makes me feel like a waiter.

MITCHELL. Well, we had to wear them tonight. No one will ever suspect what we're up to. We'll be able to lose ourselves in the crowd downstairs. (*Looking over* PAUL's *tuxedo.*) I used to have a tux like that. A long time ago.

PAUL. What's wrong with it?

MITCHELL. Nothing. On you it looks good.

PAUL. I got married in this tuxedo. Look, I still have rice in the pocket. (*Pulls out a few grains of rice and throws them to the floor.*)

MITCHELL. If only I could forget her. If only I could get Arlene out of my mind. I never thought she'd leave me, Paul.

PAUL. She's very good at leaving people.

MITCHELL. What I did for that woman. I changed my whole way of life for her. Except for that time with Judy I cut out all other women.

PAUL. I cut out potatoes.

MITCHELL. I bought her anything she wanted. You know what I got her for her birthday? . . . A grandfather clock.

PAUL. Did she like it?

MITCHELL. I guess so. She took it with her when she left. God, what I did for her, Paul. I idolized her. I worshipped her. My whole life was for her. Why would she leave me, Paul? Why?

PAUL. Can I be truthful?

MITCHELL. Sure.

PAUL. Now, I don't mean to criticize or anything, but you're a bit of a baby. A little baby.

MITCHELL. Maybe you're right. (*They both pick up the platform cover and place it in place.*) I was so depressed. I tried everything to forget her. I even went on a Caribbean cruise. Seven days and seven nights, all alone. I never left my cabin once.

PAUL. You need more than seven days and seven nights to forget Arlene. (PAUL *jumps up and down on the platform to test it.*) Not bad.

MITCHELL. Before I met Arlene I wasn't a complicated person. Now I go to group therapy five nights a week. Saturdays and Sundays I'm lost.

PAUL. That whore!

MITCHELL. That bitch!

PAUL. That slut!

(*The two of them reach Upstage behind the bed and lift up and insert into the platform, a large homemade wooden gibbet, creating a hangman's scaffold. The gibbet is about six inches wide, four inches deep and about nine feet tall with a three foot protruding arm on top from which to hang the rope.*)

MITCHELL. Do you think this thing's going to hold up?

PAUL. Who cares. We're only going to use it once. You got the rope?

MITCHELL. It's in the bag. (PAUL *goes to the shopping bag and starts to pull out the rope. It's endless.*) You know, my practice has fallen off. The other day I was taking an impression on one of my few remaining patients and I cemented her gums together.

PAUL. (*Still pulling out rope.*) How much rope did you get?

MITCHELL. Enough to do the job. Last week I did a root canal on an old man who wears false teeth.

PAUL. (*Still pulling rope.*) What did you tell them you wanted it for?

MITCHELL. What?

PAUL. The rope.

MITCHELL. Mountain climbing.

PAUL. There are no mountains around here.

MITCHELL. I got the rope, didn't I? You know what I did yesterday? I dropped a gold filling down a woman's throat. That's a hundred and forty dollars down the toilet. Paul, I'm in such pain, such torment, the sense of loss, the sense of dread. Going to bed each night because you know you're not going to sleep and then the terrible fear of waking up in the morning because you know you have nothing to get up for.

PAUL. (*Finishes pulling out the rope.*) Jesus Christ! There's gotta be a hundred feet here.

MITCHELL. I couldn't just go out and buy four feet of rope. They'd get suspicious.

PAUL. How much did this cost?

MITCHELL. (*Takes out receipt from pocket.*) Twelve-fifty. You owe me six and a quarter.

PAUL. I'll give you two bucks. The rest you can get when you take the left-over rope back to the store.

MITCHELL. I can't. I bought it on sale.

PAUL. You bought rope on sale?

MITCHELL. It's a second. There's a flaw in it.

PAUL. What kind of a flaw?

MITCHELL. How do I know? It was such a good deal. I didn't want to ask.

PAUL. A flaw. She's going to be here any minute, and I have to look for a flaw. (*He gets down on his knees and frantically looks for the flaw in the rope.*) Where's the flaw? I can't find the flaw!

MITCHELL. You know how much it's costing us to hang Arlene? Between the room, the wood, the nails and the rope, it's over a hundred dollars.

PAUL. Believe me, it's a bargain.

MITCHELL. (*Crosses to closet and opens the door.*) We could have saved a lot of money hanging her in the closet.

PAUL. No good. Her feet would have touched the floor. (*He gives up looking for the flaw and rises.*)

MITCHELL. No. Not if we tied her neck to the crossbar and her ankles to the coat hook.

PAUL. Hey, we're hanging my wife, not roasting a pig. This is the best way. (*Goes towards scaffold.* MITCHELL *follows.*) We place the noose around her neck. Then we go back here and pull for as long as it takes. The best part is we don't have to see her make all those faces.

MITCHELL. It's actually more humane that way. You want me to make the noose?

PAUL. No, I'll make the noose. I'm still her husband. There has to be some privilege that comes with it.

(*He sits on the bed and begins making noose. During the following,* MITCHELL *puts a chair on the platform, stands on it, tilts his neck and goes limp as if just hanged.*)

MITCHELL. I can almost forgive her for cheating on a husband. But how can anyone cheat on a lover? You know, you had a lot to do with this whole thing. If you hadn't talked her into going to your self-realization class, she never would have realized she didn't want either one of us. (*Gets down and goes towards bed.*)

PAUL. Of all people to wind up with her. That rotten, good for nothing teacher of mine, Malcolm Dewey.

MITCHELL. (*Correcting him.*) Malcolm Dewey Incorporated.

PAUL. Yeah, he's big business now, the little runt.

MITCHELL. You have to admit he found a great gimmick. Promising everyone the meaning of life in one month.

PAUL. The bastard's got franchises all over the country.

MITCHELL. I have a confession to make, Paul. I went for one of his five hundred dollar weekends. He doesn't even let you go to the bathroom.

PAUL. Did you get anything out of it?

MITCHELL. Yeah, kidney stones.

PAUL. I knew things were going to work out for us when I read he was holding his New Year's Eve Membership Drive in this hotel.

MITCHELL. There must be a thousand people down there in the ballroom.

PAUL. Yeah, and nine hundred of them are women.

MITCHELL. What do they see in him?

PAUL. I think he stuffs his pants.

MITCHELL. Of all the women he could have, why did he have to pick ours?

PAUL. It's a nightmare.

MITCHELL. Do you think she'll fall for the note?

PAUL. Are you kidding. Arlene's a romantic. When she gets the key to this room and my beautiful forged note she'll think it's from him and she'll be up here in a flash. That whore.

MITCHELL. That bitch.

PAUL. That slut. (*He has made the noose. He hands it to* MITCHELL.) Here. Try this. (MITCHELL *takes it, pulls one end and the noose immediately falls apart.*)

MITCHELL. What kind of noose is this?

PAUL. (*Grabbing the rope from him.*) You broke it.

MITCHELL. What do you mean I broke it? It came apart. The same thing would have happened the minute you put it around Arlene's neck.

PAUL. (*Starts making another noose.*) I tell you, Mitch, once she's dead I'll never marry again.

MITCHELL. Don't be ridiculous. Sure you will.

PAUL. No, I learned my lesson. In this day and age, marriage doesn't work anymore. Women are starting to think now. They question everything. It's no fun being married to them.

MITCHELL. Don't be silly. Married life is the only way. You have no idea how I used to envy you. Coming home every night. There was music. There was laughter.

PAUL. What about the nights she wasn't there?

MITCHELL. Then I had the music and the laughter. But you had it a lot more.

PAUL. Yeah, but in the morning when you woke up you had the bed all to yourself. You could stretch without bumping into anyone.

MITCHELL. Yeah, but on a cold night you had that warm body against you.

PAUL. Yeah, but winter isn't forever.

MITCHELL. An empty house is a lonely house.

PAUL. Maybe you should move in with your mother.

MITCHELL. I can't. She's living with someone.

PAUL. I'm telling you, Mitch, the country is sinking fast. (*A new thought.*) I was afraid to ask you this because, for a long time there, you were the enemy, but, uh, . . . did Arlene ever tell you anything about me?

MITCHELL. No, not really.

PAUL. Did she tell you I was a bad lover?

MITCHELL. No. Not in so many words.

PAUL. That whore.

MITCHELL. That bitch.

PAUL. That slut. (*Hands the noose to* MITCHELL.) Here, try this. (MITCHELL *takes the noose and pulls on it. The knot immediately comes apart again.*) You broke it again.

MITCHELL. Let me try it. I used to be a Boy Scout.

PAUL. (*Sadly.*) They wouldn't take me. (*Paces around room.*) What I did for that woman. I wanted to make her proud of me. I knew I had no class. I knew she outgrew me. I knew it because she used to tell me. So I took all kinds of courses. Sexual creativity. Psychological intertwining. Creative pottery with the feet. (*Demonstrates with one foot.*) I even took a speed reading course. And for what?

MITCHELL. Poor guy.

PAUL. I read "War and Peace" in an hour and ten minutes flat. And for what? I even took up dancing. I learned the old . . . (*Starts dancing poorly.*) One, two . . . one, two, three . . .

MITCHELL. Who do you go dancing with?

PAUL. No one. That's why I'll never be any good. You know what the irony is, Mitchell? I may have outgrown the woman who once outgrew me.

MITCHELL. Admit it, Paul. You're even more hurt than I am.

PAUL. Why shouldn't I be? I'm the one who always gets stuck with the hotel bill.

MITCHELL. (*Hands* PAUL *rope.*) Here, try this.

PAUL. (*Impressed with the noose.*) Hey, that's good. That's going to fit real tight.

MITCHELL. Have you got all the evidence?

PAUL. (*Pulls articles from under the bed and tosses them*

to MITCHELL.) Yeah. I got it here under the bed. Malcolm Dewey's cape. Malcolm Dewey's top hat. (*He pops it open.*) . . . And Malcolm Dewey's galoshes.

MITCHELL. Great. That should send that phony double-talker up the river for life.

PAUL. (*Pulls out a white silk scarf.*) And the clincher. Malcolm Dewey's white silk scarf. (*He rises.*)

MITCHELL. Paul, you are the best thief in town.

PAUL. Thank you. That's my business. And I also have this. (*Pulls out a tube of lipstick from his jacket pocket.*)

MITCHELL. Lipstick?

PAUL. Arlene's lipstick. When they find her lipstick on his scarf . . .

MITCHELL. You're brilliant, Paul.

PAUL. Thank you. (*Holds lipstick towards* MITCHELL.) Here, put on the lipstick and kiss the scarf.

MITCHELL. Pardon me?

PAUL. I said put the lipstick on and kiss the scarf.

MITCHELL. Get Arlene to kiss the scarf.

PAUL. I couldn't even get her to kiss me. I've been studying your face, Mitch. Your lips are a lot like hers. Put on the lipstick and kiss the scarf.

MITCHELL. I never put lipstick on in my life, and I'm not about to start now. I have two rules that I live by. No lipstick and no personal checks.

PAUL. Put on the lipstick and stop aggravating me.

MITCHELL. No. You put it on.

PAUL. (*Growing impatient.*) Mitch, put it on or I'm calling the whole thing off.

MITCHELL. (*Reluctantly takes lipstick, goes to imaginary Downstage mirror and starts to put it on.*) Okay, but this better not leave the room. (*He applies the lipstick very skillfully.*) How does this look?

PAUL. (*Leans his head on* MITCHELL'S *shoulder for a moment.*) I like it. (*Hands him the scarf.*) Here! Now kiss the scarf! (MITCHELL *takes the scarf and kisses it. He then hands it back to* PAUL. *Impressed.*) A perfect "o." We work very well as a team. (*He places the scarf on the bed.*)

MITCHELL. Maybe we can do other things together.

PAUL. Oh, it's going to be good with her out of the way.

(*During the following they attach the noose to the scaffold and run the rest of the rope down the back. Once they finish that they remove the chair and put away the tools.*)

MITCHELL. Say, you doing anything afterwards?

PAUL. I think I'll go home and watch Guy Lombardo.

MITCHELL. He's dead.

PAUL. (*Sighs.*) What a life.

MITCHELL. Do you like fish?

PAUL. Only if they take the bones out, why?

MITCHELL. There's a cute little place around the corner. They're open late tonight, I checked. Let me buy you dinner. It's not nice to be alone New Year's Eve.

PAUL. Well, I am dressed up.

MITCHELL. Sure, why waste it? It'll be fun. They'll give us hats and noisemakers . . .

PAUL. Okay, but we'll go dutch. And, since you got the rope, I'll get the wine.

MITCHELL. Maybe tomorrow night we can catch a movie.

PAUL. Let's see how dinner goes first.

MITCHELL. (*Putting on his tuxedo jacket.*) You know, Paul. Of all the murders planned between us, this is the best one yet.

PAUL. (*Putting on Malcolm's cape and top hat.*) That's because Arlene's not around to screw things up. One thing I'll say for him, the kid knows how to dress.

(*There is the sound of a key in the door.*)

MITCHELL. That's her.

PAUL. Shut the lights.

(MITCHELL *shuts the lights and stands away from the door.* PAUL *stands in the middle of the room.* ARLENE *enters the room tentatively leaving the door open. She walks towards* PAUL.)

ARLENE. Malcolm? . . . Malcolm?

(MITCHELL *flips the lights on just as* PAUL *spreads his cape in Dracula fashion.*)

PAUL. Happy New Year, Arlene.

ARLENE. (*Startled.*) Paul!

MITCHELL. (*Slams the door shut.*) Hi, Arlene. How's tricks?

ARLENE. Mitchell! All right, what's going on here? I was supposed to meet Malcolm Dewey.

PAUL. Malcolm Dewey is through-ie. (MITCHELL *removes the doorknob with a screwdriver.*)

ARLENE. (*Looking at scaffold.*) I think I deserve an explanation.

PAUL. Bad news, Arlene. You're starting off the New Year dead. What you did to us, there's no excuse. Two men who loved you desperately. (*She starts for the door.*)

MITCHELL. (*Holding up doorknob.*) Don't bother, Arlene. I've got the doorknob.

PAUL. And don't bother screaming either. It's New Year's Eve. We've been hammering for hours and no one's complained. (*He screams to demonstrate. So does* MITCHELL. ARLENE *screams for real.*) Hear any complaints? (*He removes the top hat and cape.*)

ARLENE. I don't understand. I was downstairs helping to register new members, then I got this note from Malcolm with a key asking me to meet him here.

MITCHELL. Paul wrote that note.

ARLENE. (*To* PAUL.) You! But the handwriting is just like his.

PAUL. I spent months and months perfecting it.

MITCHELL. It put us behind schedule. We were planning to kill you on Halloween.

ARLENE. (*Notices* MITCHELL's *lips.*) Mitchell, are you wearing lipstick?

MITCHELL. Oh. (*He starts wiping it off.* ARLENE *looks from one to the other.*)

PAUL. It's not what you think, Arlene. (*Indicates* MALCOLM's *belongings.*) Look, Arlene, do you recognize any of this?

ARLENE. Malcolm's cape. Malcolm's top hat. Malcolm's galoshes. Malcolm's scarf.

PAUL. (*Holding scarf towards her.*) Do these lips look familiar?

ARLENE. Those are my lips.

MITCHELL. (*Proudly.*) Wrong, those are *my* lips.

ARLENE. (*To* PAUL.) What are you doing with his things?

PAUL. Very simple, Arlene. A; we're going to hang you. B; we're going to pin it on Malcolm . . .

MITCHELL. And C; we're going to open up this bottle of champagne and celebrate.

ARLENE. You'll never get away with this. Malcolm's downstairs with a thousand witnesses. He has the perfect alibi.

PAUL. All taken care of. The minute we hang you, we call downstairs and tell him there's a rich investor in Room Ten Fifteen.

MITCHELL. We leave, he comes up, we call the cops, they catch him here with your dead body and I guarantee you his alibi is worth less than one of Paul's warranties.

PAUL. Let's hang her. (*They drag her to the scaffold.*)

ARLENE. Come on, fellas. Be reasonable.

PAUL. Get up there, you harlot.

MITCHELL. Harlot? I haven't heard that one in a while.

ARLENE. You can't hang an innocent woman.

PAUL. Innocent? You stand on a scaffold and call yourself innocent? Innocent is a wife who checks into a Howard Johnson's with her husband.

MITCHELL. Or her first lover.

PAUL. Right.

MITCHELL. Arlene, why? Why a third guy?

PAUL. How could you leave us for a twenty five year old snot nose millionaire?

MITCHELL. A kid who wears galoshes.

PAUL. He's a foot shorter than you and has a head the size of a basketball.

MITCHELL. And so skinny. Naked he must look like a grapefruit on a stick.

PAUL. Was it strictly sex? Could he be that much better than us?

ARLENE. Sex? Do you think I left you for sex? Do you think all that's on my mind is sex?

PAUL. Arlene, cut the crap. You're talking to a used car dealer.

ARLENE. Paul, a woman doesn't leave her husband and her lover for sex.

PAUL. Yes, she does.

ARLENE. No, she doesn't.

MITCHELL. Yes, she does.

ARLENE. No, she doesn't. Paul, with you I was able to fulfill my wifely instincts and Mitchell, with you, I was able to fulfill my sexual instincts. But with Malcolm I'm on a whole new plateau. A much higher plane. I've expanded my vision.

PAUL. Arlene, are you on dope?

ARLENE. With Malcolm it's very different. We think together. We delve. We probe. We search. We seek.

MITCHELL. Paul thinks he stuffs his pants. You mean to say you never ever had sex with Malcolm Dewey?

ARLENE. Never!

PAUL. No sex?

ARLENE. Not even once.

MITCHELL. Arlene, was Malcolm ever in a hunting accident?

ARLENE. Malcolm taught me to be free. To escape the same mundane, every day, going nowhere, learning nothing, terminal middle class life.

PAUL. Having a husband and a lover is middle class?

MITCHELL. If that's middle class, I wonder what the rich are doing.

ARLENE. Malcolm took me beyond the realm of the senses into a world of inner space. We no longer use words like love and caring. It is nothing but human vanity to feel compassion for your fellow man. In order to attain completion it is better for mankind to be totally selfish. Don't you understand what he's done? Malcolm has made me more than a woman. I'm a movement.

PAUL. Arlene, we're not just hanging you. We're hanging an idea. A very dangerous idea. I'm not sure what that idea is, but I know it's trouble. I'm not saying a woman's place is in the home. I'm past that. We're all past that today. But to leave two terrific guys like us for someone who just talks to you, that's sick and you gotta be destroyed.

PAUL. *(Tightening the rope around ARLENE's neck.)* How does that feel?

ARLENE. A little tight.

PAUL. Good.

MITCHELL. *(To ARLENE.)* Any last words before we hang you?

ARLENE. Yes, don't hang me.

MITCHELL. That's an old joke, Arlene.

PAUL. Let's get this over with. *(They go behind the*

scaffold and take hold of the rope.)

ARLENE. Your hanging me tonight will not stop the wave of selfishness that's rippling across the country.

PAUL and MITCHELL. One!

ARLENE. Sure, you'll get rid of me. But don't you think there are others to carry the torch?

PAUL and MITCHELL. Two!

ARLENE. There isn't enough rope in the world to stop this avalanche of self-indulgence.

PAUL and MITCHELL. Three!

ARLENE. You cannot hang a dream!

PAUL and MITCHELL. Goodbye, Arlene!

(They pull the rope. It snaps and they fall backwards. NOTE: This is done by means of a second rope that has been rigged to the hack of the gibbet.)

PAUL. The flaw! I found the flaw! *(ARLENE immediately runs to the door, forgetting there's no doorknob.)* Get her!

ARLENE. *(She turns and goes towards bed.) You'll* never get me. *(ARLENE dives under the bed.)*

PAUL. Get her! Get her!

MITCHELL. Right! *(MITCHELL crawls under the bed after ARLENE.)*

PAUL. Shafted by rope. *(A beat.)* Have you got her? *(There is silence.)* Have you got her? *(Still no answer. He looks under the bed.)* You're like animals. Get out of there. I' ll get a pail of cold water. *(Gets up, opens bathroom door, looks in.)* There's never a bucket when you need one. A stick. I'll get a stick. *(Goes to closet and takes down cross bar and goes to bed and pokes underneath.)* Come on. Get out from under there.

MITCHELL. Oooow! *(MITCHELL and ARLENE*

come out from under the bed.) You're still the sexiest woman I ever met, Arlene.

ARLENE. I forgot what a good kisser you are.

PAUL. That does it. I've had it. The hell with the hanging. I'm going to strangle you with my bare hands. *(ARLENE and MITCHELL rise. PAUL goes towards ARLENE. He has a maniacal look on his face.)* My suffering days are over. I'm through having to worry about where you are, who you're with, what you're doing. That's it. It's over. Finished. *(He throws ARLENE on the bed, kneels over her and begins strangling her. MITCHELL, aware of the seriousness of the situation heads towards the door.)* You know why I'm killing you, Arlene? Not because you made my life a shambles, but because I'm going to enjoy it. And I'm going to get away with it. Do you know why? Because thanks to you, I'm now insane. *(Laughs fiendishly.) You* made me insane, Arlene. And when I'm through with her, Mitch, I'm strangling you. *(MITCHELL quickly gets the doorknob and starts screwing it into the door. PAUL gets up from bed.)* And then when you're dead, Mitch, you know who's next? Me. I'm strangling myself. In fact, I may start with me first. *(He starts choking himself. Suddenly he clutches his chest in pain.)* Ooooooooooh!

ARLENE. *(Concerned. She rushes to him.)* Paul!

MITCHELL. *(Also concerned. Goes to him.)* What's wrong? *(PAUL outlines the shape of a heart with his finger and then points to his chest.)*

ARLENE. I think he's having a heart attack.

MITCHELL. Oh, no.

ARLENE. Help him! Help him! Quick, lay him down. *(They help PAUL to the bed. MITCHELL gets some pillows to put behind him.)* Hurry! Get him a doctor.

MITCHELL. I'm a doctor. *(To PAUL, examining his*

mouth.) Open up. *(PAUL opens his mouth wide.)*

ARLENE. No, you're a dentist. Get him a real doctor.

MITCHELL. *(To ARLENE.)* Get him some water. I'll call the desk.

ARLENE. Right. *(Rushes Off to the bathroom. MITCHELL picks up phone, PAUL grabs his hand.)*

PAUL. Mitch! Wait. If anything happens to me, promise me you'll take care of her.

MITCHELL. You mean, hang her myself?

PAUL. No, I mean take care of her. See that she keeps out of trouble.

ARLENE. *(Comes running out with a glass of water.)* Don't die, Paul. Don't die.

PAUL. Give me the water.

ARLENE. Here, sweetheart. *(She tries to put it in his mouth but it goes all over his face.)*

PAUL. Not in my face. In my mouth.

ARLENE. *(To MITCHELL.)* Did you get the Doctor?

MITCHELL. I'm trying. *(Into phone.)* Hello? . . . Who's this? *(To PAUL and ARLENE.)* I got room service. Do you want to order anything? *(MITCHELL tries dialing another number.)*

PAUL. *(To ARLENE.)* I'm sorry for the inconvenience I caused you by being married to you. My whole life has been a series of inconveniences. Things have always gone wrong for me. I'm a loser. It's as simple as that. That's all I've ever been.

MITCHELL. No, you're not. You're a very decent person, Paul. I'd hate to think what would have happened to me if I had screwed around with anybody else's wife.

PAUL. I could have been nicer.

MITCHELL. *(Into phone.)* Hello? . . . Hello? . . .

Who's this? *(To PAUL and ARLENE.)* It's reservations. Anybody want to come back here?

PAUL. Nothing goes right for Paul Miller. I've never come out on top. Just once, I would have liked to have had a good laugh out of life.

MITCHELL. Did you hear the one about the nun and the midget?

PAUL. *(Gasping for air.)* It's too late, Mitch. Don't bother. It wasn't meant to be. It wasn't written in the stars. I'm checking out. That's it, I'm cashing in my chips. Just a minute, I think it's passing. I think I'm okay.

ARLENE. What?

PAUL. I think I'm all right. I think it was just gas. Wow, I saw death again. It remembered me. *(MITCHELL hangs up the phone.)*

ARLENE. What did you eat for lunch?

PAUL. It's not what I eat. It's how I eat. I eat too fast lately. Rushing, running, planning murders . . . Why do we make things so difficult for ourselves? Why do we have to keep trying to kill each other? We're no good at it.

MITCHELL. We're awful. *(Gets champagne and the two glasses.)*

ARLENE. It's all my fault. I didn't know what I wanted. I confused you both.

(During the following, MITCHELL pops open the champagne, pours glass for ARLENE and himself. He then pours some into PAUL's bathroom glass. He accidentally misses the glass. It goes all over PAUL's pants. Nobody acknowledges it.)

MITCHELL. No, no. It's my fault. If I hadn't come

into the picture . . .

PAUL. No, it's my fault. For holding on so much. I wouldn't let go.

ARLENE. No, I'm the guilty party in this whole mess.

MITCHELL. No, no. I'm much more guilty than you.

PAUL. We're all guilty.

ARLENE. No one is as guilty as Malcolm Dewey. When I thought you were dying just now I realized how wrong he's been about the meaning of life. People have got to care for each other.

MITCHELL. He's made this a rotten year for all three of us.

PAUL. The two bit phony is a menace to decent citizens like us.

ARLENE. Well, I'm starting this New Year on the right foot. Paul, I'm coming back to you.

PAUL. Arlene, you'll never regret it. We'll work at it together. We may never find happiness but maybe we'll find something close.

MTTCHELL. And this time I'm staying out of it. I've learned my lesson. I'm going to be your dentist and that's all. *(Looks at watch.)* Hey, it's almost midnight.

ARLENE. Quick, turn on the TV. We can watch the ball come down on Times Square. *(MITCHELL clicks the set on.)* Oh, boy. Another year gone by.

MITCHELL. It sure flew, didn't it?

PAUL. I get the feeling this one will be better. *(The set goes on. The three countdown.)*

ARLENE, PAUL and MITCHELL. Nine . . . Eight . . . Seven . . . Six . . . Five . . . Four . . . Three . . . Two . . . One.

ARLENE. *(To PAUL.)* Happy New Year, darling.

PAUL. Happy New Year, Mitch. *(ARLENE kisses PAUL. PAUL shakes MITCHELL's hand.)* Happy New Year, Mitch.

MITCHELL. Happy New Year, Paul.

(ARLENE and MITCHELL kiss, The three look at the TV and join in singing "AULD LANG SYNE." Slowly ARLENE and MITCHELL turn to each other and kiss passionately. PAUL still singing, realizes he's singing by himself, looks over at them, looks at the audience, looks at them again and then continues singing.)

(SLOW CURTAIN BEGINS TO FALL.)

THE END

NOTE: The permanent set (see Ground Plan) is as follows—

CLOSET, Downstage Right
BATHROOM, Upstage of closet
BED WITH HIGH HEADBOARD, Upstage Right
BED-TABLE, each side of bed
THREE WINDOWS, Upstage—Left to Right
LOW, NARROW PLATFORM outside windows (For "walk-around")
HALL DOOR, Stage Right

SPECIAL NOTES: Windows should pivot on their centers in frames.

PROPERTY LIST

ACT ONE, SCENE 1—On Stage
towel, hanging bar (in closet)
necktie (closet doorknob)
telephone (Stage Right bed table)
blue headboard (bed)
Xmas wreath (headboard)
hard chair (Right of bed)
Bible (Left side bed table)
blue bed spread
2 pillows, blanket, sheets
waste basket (Upstage Left of bed)
blue curtains (2/3 open)
desk (front of Center window)
blue lamp (Right on desk)
tray, pitcher, 4 glasses (Center on desk)
luggage rack (front of Left window)
ARLENE's purse (Right of luggage rack)
shopping bag with Xmas gifts (Center on luggage rack)
castered desk chair
ARLENE's coat (hook, Upstage of hall door)
MITCH's coat (hook, Upstage of hall door)
"Do Not Disturb" sign (inside doorknob)
room # "514" (outside hall door)
TV and table (Downstage Left)
floor lamp (Left of Center)
2 armchairs (1 each side of floor lamp)
assorted hotel menus, "tents," and literature
PRESET: mattress and quilts (For "Jump"—Scene 1-2); postcard and pen (desk) for Scene 1-2; doorknob "pin" (removed for Act Two, previous performance)

Off Right (Bathroom)
doctor's bag with hypo needle, dental instruments, dentist's jacket

gag towel
shower curtain
2 towels
man's hair brush
ARLENE's wig and shawl

Off Left
man's 'kerchief
Xmas wrapped watch

ACT ONE, SCENE 2—On Stage
gold headboard (bed)
gold bed spread
gold curtains (2/3 open)
red, white and blue festoon (headboard) strike Xmas wreath
ARLENE's purse with gun, Kleenex, sleeping pills (foot of bed)
desk lamp, red—strike blue lamp
strike floor lamp
set low, round table between 2 armchairs (Left of Center)
Door # "907"—outside hall door
strike PAUL's hat and overcoat

Off Right
gun shot and cover gun

Off Left
brown paper bag with beer six-pack, bucket of fried chicken legs
long paper bag with bottle of "Blue Nun" wine

ACT TWO—On Stage
clear closet
check removable closet bar
TV remote control—Right bed table
red bed spread
red headboard
"Happy New Year" sign—headboard (strike red, white and blue)

telephone—Stage Left bed table
man's white scarf, top hat, old-fashioned galoshes, black cape with bright red lining—all under bed
red curtains (closed)
desk lamp, cream (strike red)
bottle of champagne, 2 glasses—Left on desk
check desk chair—*no casters*
strike luggage rack
gibbet—with head under Upstage side of bed—with breakaway rope
scaffold frame-base, Left of Center
top of frame base (against Stage Left wall)
screwdriver (ledge, Stage Left wall)
MITCHELL's jacket (hook Upstage of hall door)
Room #1015—(outside hall door)
remove pin from doorknob
hammer and nails (on floor near scaffold frame)
check TV: "On" switch, sound, video (if used)
strike "Do Not Disturb" sign, 2 armchairs, table
check—shopping bag with 100′ of nylon rope (Downstage of bed)

Off Right
towel (bathroom)
glass of water

Off Left
sales slip (rope purchase)
lipstick (PAUL)
envelope with note and key

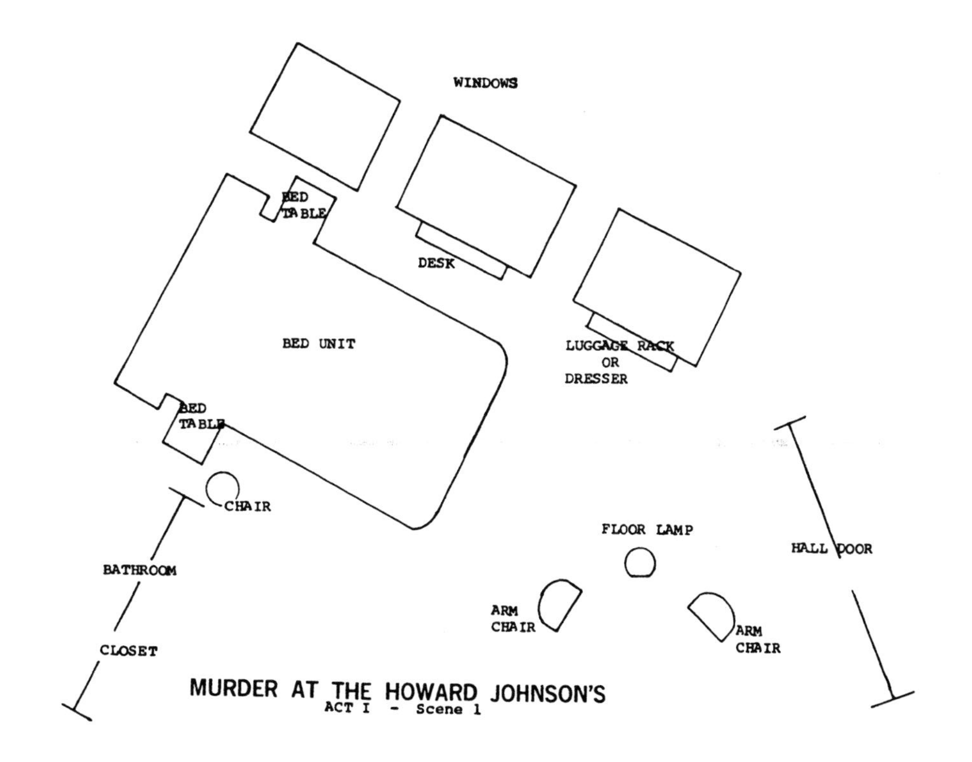
WINDOWS
BED TABLE
DESK
BED UNIT
LUGGAGE RACK OR DRESSER
BED TABLE
CHAIR
FLOOR LAMP
HALL DOOR
BATHROOM
ARM CHAIR
ARM CHAIR
CLOSET
MURDER AT THE HOWARD JOHNSON'S
ACT I - Scene 1

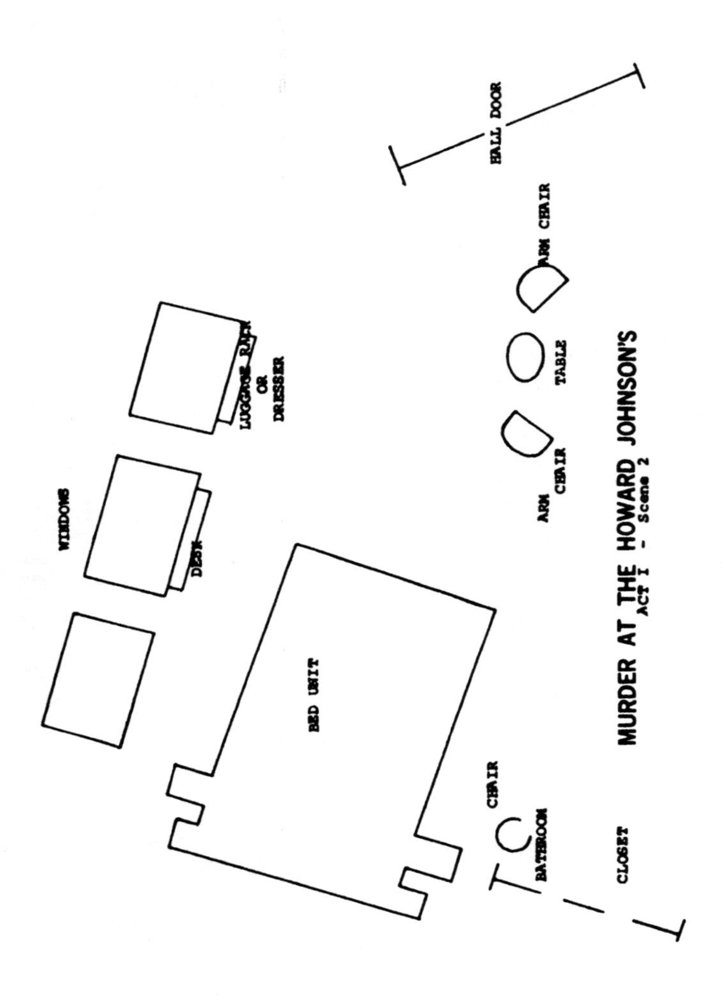
HALL DOOR
ARM CHAIR
TABLE
ARM CHAIR
LUGGAGE
OR
DRESSER
WINDOWS
DESK
BED UNIT
CHAIR
BATHROOM
CLOSET
MURDER AT THE HOWARD JOHNSON'S
ACT I - Scene 2

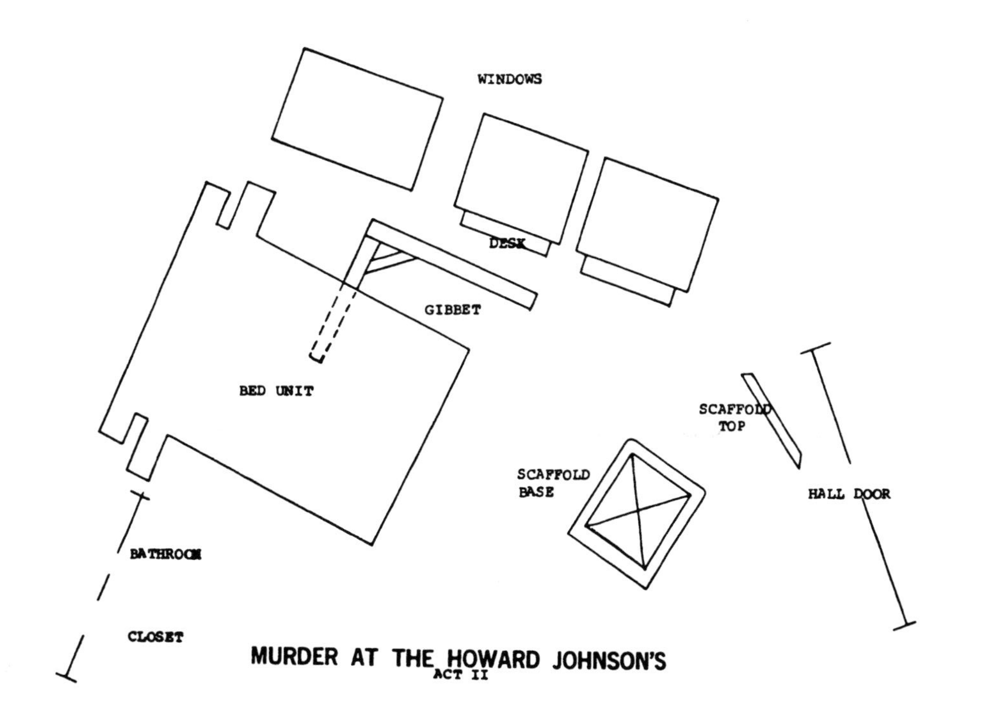
WINDOWS
DESK
GIBBET
BED UNIT
SCAFFOLD TOP
SCAFFOLD BASE
HALL DOOR
BATHROOM
CLOSET
MURDER AT THE HOWARD JOHNSON'S
ACT II

SKIN DEEP
Jon Lonoff

Comedy / 2m, 2f / Interior Unit Set

In *Skin Deep*, a large, lovable, lonely-heart, named Maureen Mulligan, gives romance one last shot on a blind-date with sweet awkward Joseph Spinelli; she's learned to pepper her speech with jokes to hide insecurities about her weight and appearance, while he's almost dangerously forthright, saying everything that comes to his mind. They both know they're perfect for each other, and in time they come to admit it.

They were set up on the date by Maureen's sister Sheila and her husband Squire, who are having problems of their own: Sheila undergoes a non-stop series of cosmetic surgeries to hang onto the attractive and much-desired Squire, who may or may not have long ago held designs on Maureen, who introduced him to Sheila. With Maureen particularly vulnerable to both hurting and being hurt, the time is ripe for all these unspoken issues to bubble to the surface.

"Warm-hearted comedy … the laughter was literally show-stopping. A winning play, with enough good-humored laughs and sentiment to keep you smiling from beginning to end."
– *TalkinBroadway.com*

"It's a little Paddy Chayefsky, a lot Neil Simon and a quick-witted, intelligent voyage into the not-so-tranquil seas of middle-aged love and dating. The dialogue is crackling and hilarious; the plot simple but well-turned; the characters endearing and quirky; and lurking beneath the merriment is so much heartache that you'll stand up and cheer when the unlikely couple makes it to the inevitable final clinch."
– *NYTheatreWorld.Com*

COCKEYED
William Missouri Downs

Comedy / 3m, 1f / Unit Set

Phil, an average nice guy, is madly in love with the beautiful Sophia. The only problem is that she's unaware of his existence. He tries to introduce himself but she looks right through him. When Phil discovers Sophia has a glass eye, he thinks that might be the problem, but soon realizes that she really can't see him. Perhaps he is caught in a philosophical hyperspace or dualistic reality or perhaps beautiful women are just unaware of nice guys. Armed only with a B.A. in philosophy, Phil sets out to prove his existence and win Sophia's heart. This fast moving farce is the winner of the HotCity Theatre's GreenHouse New Play Festival. The St. Louis Post-Dispatch called Cockeyed a clever romantic comedy, Talkin' Broadway called it "hilarious," while Playback Magazine said that it was "fresh and invigorating."

Winner!
of the HotCity Theatre GreenHouse New Play Festival

"Rocking with laughter...hilarious...polished and engaging work draws heavily on the age-old conventions of farce: improbable situations, exaggerated characters, amazing coincidences, absurd misunderstandings, people hiding in closets and barely missing each other as they run in and out of doors...full of comic momentum as Cockeyed hurtles toward its conclusion."
–Talkin' Broadway

THE OFFICE PLAYS

Two full length plays by Adam Bock

THE RECEPTIONIST

Comedy / 2m, 2f / Interior

At the start of a typical day in the Northeast Office, Beverly deals effortlessly with ringing phones and her colleague's romantic troubles. But the appearance of a charming rep from the Central Office disrupts the friendly routine. And as the true nature of the company's business becomes apparent, The Receptionist raises disquieting, provocative questions about the consequences of complicity with evil.

"...Mr. Bock's poisoned Post-it note of a play."
– *New York Times*

"Bock's intense initial focus on the routine goes to the heart of *The Receptionist's* pointed, painfully timely allegory... elliptical, provocative play..."
– *Time Out New York*

THE THUGS

Comedy / 2m, 6f / Interior

The Obie Award winning dark comedy about work, thunder and the mysterious things that are happening on the 9th floor of a big law firm. When a group of temps try to discover the secrets that lurk in the hidden crevices of their workplace, they realize they would rather believe in gossip and rumors than face dangerous realities.

"Bock starts you off giggling, but leaves you with a chill."
– *Time Out New York*

"... a delightfully paranoid little nightmare that is both more chillingly realistic and pointedly absurd than anything John Grisham ever dreamed up."
– *New York Times*

ANON
Kate Robin

Drama / 2m, 12f / Area

Anon. follows two couples as they cope with sexual addiction. Trip and Allison are young and healthy, but he's more interested in his abnormally large porn collection than in her. While they begin to work through both of their own sexual and relationship hang-ups, Trip's parents are stuck in the roles they've been carving out for years in their dysfunctional marriage. In between scenes with these four characters, 10 different women, members of a support group for those involved with individuals with sex addiction issues, tell their stories in monologues that are alternately funny and harrowing..

In addition to Anon., Robin's play What They Have was also commissioned by South Coast Repertory. Her plays have also been developed at Manhattan Theater Club, Playwrights Horizons, New York Theatre Workshop, The Eugene O'Neill Theater Center's National Playwrights Conference, JAW/West at Portland Center Stage and Ensemble Studio Theatre. Television and film credits include "Six Feet Under" (writer/supervising producer) and "Coming Soon." Robin received the 2003 Princess Grace Statuette for playwriting and is an alumna of New Dramatists.

WHITE BUFFALO
Don Zolidis

Drama / 3m, 2f (plus chorus)/ Unit Set

Based on actual events, WHITE BUFFALO tells the story of the miracle birth of a white buffalo calf on a small farm in southern Wisconsin. When Carol Gelling discovers that one of the buffalo on her farm is born white in color, she thinks nothing more of it than a curiosity. Soon, however, she learns that this is the fulfillment of an ancient prophecy believed by the Sioux to bring peace on earth and unity to all mankind. Her little farm is quickly overwhelmed with religious pilgrims, bringing her into contact with a culture and faith that is wholly unfamiliar to her. When a mysterious businessman offers to buy the calf for two million dollars, Carol is thrown into doubt about whether to profit from the religious beliefs of others or to keep true to a spirituality she knows nothing about.

BLUE YONDER

Kate Aspengren

Dramatic Comedy / Monolgues and scenes

12f (can be performed with as few as 4 with doubling) / Unit Set

A familiar adage states, "Men may work from sun to sun, but women's work is never done." In BIue Yonder, the audience meets twelve mesmerizing and eccentric women including a flight instructor, a firefighter, a stuntwoman, a woman who donates body parts, an employment counselor, a professional softball player, a surgical nurse professional baseball player, and a daredevil who plays with dynamite among others. Through the monologues, each woman examines her life's work and explores the career that she has found. Or that has found her.